"Maybe God sent Adam Dalton for you, Mommy,"

little Heather said.

"No," Angela responded with a soft laugh. "Mommy isn't asking for a man in her life."

"But you've been alone a long time. Wouldn't you like somebody to keep you company?" the six-year-old persisted.

"I'm fine with just you and your brothers," Angela told her small daughter. "Good night, sweetie."

Angela closed Heather's bedroom door and leaned against it. What would she do if someone like Adam Dalton entered her life now, threatening her newly found independence? She winced at the thought.

"Oh, Lord," she whispered, half in humor and half in desperation, "*please* don't send me another man...."

Books by Kathryn Alexander

Love Inspired

The Reluctant Bride #18
A Wedding in the Family #42

KATHRYN ALEXANDER

writes inspirational romance because, having been a Christian for many years, incorporating the element of faith in the Lord into a romantic story line seemed like a lovely and appropriate idea. After all, in a society where love for a lifetime is difficult to find, imagine discovering it, unexpectedly, as a gift sent from God.

Married to Kelly, her own personal love of a lifetime, Kathryn and her husband have one son, John, who is the proud owner of the family's two house pests, Herbie the cat and Copper the dog.

Kathryn and her family have been members of their church for nearly five years, where she co-teaches a Sunday school class of active two-year-olds. She is now a stay-at-home mom who writes between car pooling, baby-sitting and applying bandages, when necessary.

A Wedding in the Family

Kathryn Alexander

Published by Steeple Hill Books™

STEEPLE HILL BOOKS

ISBN 0-373-87042-6

A WEDDING IN THE FAMILY

This edition published by arrangement with Steeple Hill Books.

Printed in U.S.A.

I lift up my eyes to the hills—
where does my help come from?
My help comes from the Lord,
the Maker of heaven and earth.

—*Psalm* 121:1-2

To Mom, for her love and unending encouragement
throughout the years,
and to Grandma, for everything, always.

Chapter One

The ringing doorbell awakened Angela, more from its persistence than from its volume. She sat up on the sofa she had occupied almost from the moment she arrived home from work, and pushed her hair back from her forehead.

"I'm coming, I'm coming," she called out with a cough to the unexpected visitor. The cold that had plagued her throughout much of the week had finally won the battle, forcing Angela to admit that she was sick and that, like it or not, she needed some rest.

The impatient ringing continued, even as she opened the front door.

"Yes, what is it?" she asked in a scratchy voice when she finally pulled open the heavy wooden door of her apartment.

"Mom?! Where were you?!" cried a little dark-haired girl who rushed immediately into Angela's arms, burying her tearstained face in her mother's soft sweatshirt.

"Heather? What's the matter? What happened?" Angela quickly asked, looking from her six-year-old daughter into the frowning face of the tall, lean figure standing nearby. "What's wrong with her? What did you do—"

"What I 'did' was bring her home safely to you." His interruption was harsh, and his words spoken sharply. "I found her sitting on the curb in the dark outside the recreation center—all alone and crying. Is that your usual practice? To leave a little girl wondering if she's going to have a ride home from her swimming lesson?"

"No, of course not," Angela replied. "I couldn't pick her up tonight because I'm sick, so I made arrangements—"

"Your 'arrangements' didn't work out. No one showed up. I had just locked the office and was leaving for the night when I saw her sitting there, crying. Didn't you notice it was getting late? Swimming lessons have been over for more than an hour. She should have been home long before this." Eyes of gunmetal gray glared at her in bridled anger.

Who was this man who had delivered her child to her front door and now stood accusing her of negligence? Something about him seemed familiar.

"I was asleep...I've been sick—" Angela suddenly felt much sicker, realizing what might have happened to her daughter if this man hadn't played the role of the Good Samaritan. And Eric—how could he forget to pick up his niece? She had asked him only hours earlier. "I did hear the phone ring a while ago, but I didn't reach it in time. Maybe—"

"Don't you own an answering machine?"

"Yes, but it's broken. As of this morning." When her son, David, had accidently knocked it off the microwave.

"Well, buy a new one. That call you missed was from Heather. I took her into my office to call you so she could tell you who was bringing her home. You know, it's not a wise move to tell someone else's kid to get into your vehicle so you can take them somewhere without the parent's permission. I didn't like the idea of the possible accusations you could bring against me if this whole thing ended in misunderstanding. If you'd had an answering machine on, she could have left a message—"

"Who are you, anyway?" Angela demanded between deep coughs, suddenly feeling defensive. "I *don't* like the idea of my daughter getting into a car so willingly with a stranger."

"Adam is not a stranger, Mom. He's at swimming lessons every Thursday."

That's where she'd seen him. Once or twice when she'd picked up Heather after her class, this man had been there at the far end of the pool, talking with the children and watching their dives.

"I'm not a stranger to your daughter, Mrs. Sanders, but she really doesn't know me well enough to have agreed to come with me as easily as she did. I think you need to discuss that with her. And if you and your husband can't get your act together about transportation for her any better than you did tonight, then keep Heather home where she's safe—not sitting alone at the center at 9:00 p.m."

How could this woman have been so careless? Adam wondered as he stood looking at Angela. She certainly appeared to be the loving, motherly type.

"Her uncle should have picked her up. I'll get in touch with him tonight to find out what happened." She offered her remark quietly, humiliated and frightened to think that this had happened, that Heather had been in such a potentially dangerous predicament, that this man she didn't really know had lashed out at her so contemptuously, so angrily...and so accurately. "Thank you, very much, for bringing her home, Mr...."

"Dalton. Adam Dalton. I'm the director at the center."

Angela coughed again. "Well, thank you, Mr. Dalton. I've been ill this week, and I was asleep when you arrived, so I had no idea of the time. Hours could have passed before I realized that my brother hadn't brought Heather home. If you hadn't been there to help...." She stopped abruptly, gripped with the thought of some stranger taking her little girl away. Her eyes burned with tears and her congested head seemed to pound with the beginnings of a furious headache.

"You're welcome, Mrs. Sanders. And I hope I never need to help you in this manner again," he stated briskly, the chill in his voice not warming one bit. Then he turned to leave.

"Goodbye, Adam. Thanks for rescuing me," Heather stated rather matter-of-factly, bringing the hint of a smile to Adam's face as he looked and winked.

"See ya next week," he said as he left.

"He did save you from a dangerous situation," Angela commented, giving her child a fierce hug and ushering her inside the apartment. Angela locked the front door securely, suddenly very conscious of safety. "But we really need to thank the Lord, too. I pray for your safety every day, and I'm so grateful to Him for watching over you." Angela walked into the kitchen and picked up the telephone receiver to dial her younger brother's number. She wondered when she'd have time to buy a new answering machine to replace the broken one on the counter by her elbow. Maybe after school tomorrow.

"Do you pray for the boys, too?" Heather asked.

"Absolutely. You've prayed with me enough to know that I do." Angela listened to the rings, waiting for Eric or Hope to pick up.

"Did you pray for Daddy?" came Heather's next question.

Angela looked into the crystal-blue eyes of her inquisitive daughter, wondering how to give the complicated answer to such a simple question. Then the doorbell rang again. And again.

"Angela?" a voice called.

"It's Uncle Eric," Heather said, and rushed to open the front door.

"Heather! I'm so glad you're home! What happened? Who picked you up?" Eric was inside the door, hugging his niece.

"What happened to *you?*" Angela asked. "How could you forget to—"

"I didn't forget her," Eric explained quickly. "I got stuck in traffic. A semi overturned causing a chemical spill on the highway, and they wouldn't let anyone through. Finally, they rerouted us, and I went straight to the center—but Heather was already gone. Did you pick her up?"

"No, Adam Dalton brought her home. He works at the center, and he found her waiting alone on the curb."

"I'm sorry, Angela, but there was nothing I could do—"

"It's all right," she assured between coughs. "Heather's home. She's fine." Angela pulled a cough drop from the pocket of her sweatpants and popped it into her mouth. "I'm just so thankful Mr. Dalton cared enough to see that she made it home safely."

"Adam is nice, Mom," Heather commented.

"I'm sure he is, hon," Angela remarked. Although he had certainly not exhibited that quality toward herself, she had glimpsed it when he'd said "goodbye" to her daughter.

"Well, again, I'm sorry, Angela. Hope and the girls are waiting in the car, and I want to get back out there to tell them Heather is okay. Hope is so upset with me for running late, you'd think I caused that chemical spill myself."

"Can't Cassie and Carrie come in for a while?" Heather asked.

"Your cousins will probably catch my cold if they do," Angela said.

"Are you still feeling so sick? I talked to Mom and Dad, and they said they're keeping the boys tonight so you could rest. I could take Heather home with me—"

"No, thanks. We'll be fine here together." Angela slipped an arm around her daughter and pulled her close. After this evening, she wasn't certain she'd ever let Heather out of her sight again. At least, not until the girl turned thirty. "We'll see you later."

"Okay, good night," he called as he left. And Angela, once again, locked the front door.

"Time for bed, sweetheart," Angela said. "Go get into your pajamas."

"But what about my bath?"

"It's late, and I feel awful. Let's skip the bath tonight."

Within minutes, Angela and Heather were kneeling beside Heather's bed with the colorful butterfly-design bedspread.

"We really need to thank the Lord for taking care of you tonight."

Heather nodded. "'When I am afraid, I will trust in you,'" she quoted. "Psalm 56:3. That's my memory verse for Sunday School this week."

Angela smiled, then sneezed. She grabbed a tissue

from the flower-printed box at the side of the bed. "You trusted Him, and He did take care of you."

"Yes. I prayed for God to send someone—someone I knew, not a stranger—to take me home. And he sent Adam."

"Yes, He did," Angela agreed, then added, "So, let's thank Him for that."

After several minutes of prayer, Heather climbed between the sheets and pulled her bedspread up to her chin.

Angela kissed her daughter's forehead and turned to leave. "See you in the morning, sweetheart."

"Mom?"

"Yes, hon?"

"You didn't answer my question about Dad. Did you pray for *him?*"

Angela sighed. Sometimes the truth hurt. "I did in the beginning, Heather. A lot. But towards the end…after he left, no, I guess I didn't. At least, not much. And I regret that."

"Do you think he is in heaven?"

"If he asked the Lord to forgive him for his sins, then he's in heaven."

"Sylvia, too?"

Sylvia. A woman Angela had every reason to hate, but never found it in her heart to do so. "Yes. God forgives everyone who wants His forgiveness."

"Even if they didn't want it until the last thing before they died?" At the sight of Heather's doubting frown, her mother gave a smile of attempted comfort.

"Yes, even if it was the last thing they ever asked

for, God wouldn't say 'no.'" She walked back over to Heather's bed, leaned down and gave the girl another kiss—cold germs and all—on the forehead. "Don't worry about Dad. He wouldn't want you to do that. Now, try to get some sleep."

"Mom?"

"Hmm?"

"Maybe God wasn't just taking care of me tonight. Maybe He sent Adam for you, too."

"No," she responded somewhere between a soft laugh and a cough. "God sent Adam Dalton for you. Mommy isn't asking for a man in her life."

"But you've been alone a long time. Wouldn't you like to have somebody?"

"I'm fine here with you and your brothers. I do not need any more than that," she stated emphatically. "Good night, Heather."

Angela closed the door and leaned against it momentarily. "Oh, Lord, please don't send me another man," she whispered, half in humor and half in desperation. What would she do if someone like Adam Dalton entered her life now, threatening her newly found independence? She winced at the thought.

She had, only months earlier, received one of the surprises of a lifetime. Freedom. After nearly twelve years of a troubled marriage, her husband had finally chosen his alcoholic's life-style over a future with her, and he had found someone named Sylvia to share it with him. So Angela was free. Suddenly and unexpectedly.

And she had been the one with the unpleasant task

of explaining it all to the children: Nathan, 12, David, 10 and Heather, 6. Little did she know that her discussion with them concerning the divorce would be easy compared to the news she would have to deliver several weeks later. News that their father was gone—forever. A car accident had claimed the lives of both Dan Sanders and his girlfriend, Sylvia.

Angela thought briefly of how she had openly wept at Dan's funeral. Several people had commented in surprise that after all that had happened she still loved Dan enough to cry for him. But she didn't. She just loved her kids, and they had lost their dad. And those three sad faces broke Angela's heart—more completely than all those difficult years with Dan had ever done.

She walked into the small kitchen area and opened the cabinet over the sink in search of cold medicine. She wanted to be able to work tomorrow—Friday. There was so much to do in her new job as principal, and she needed to be there—sick or not. She swallowed the medication and drank a large glass of water to get rid of the taste. Then she headed for her own bedroom.

Tomorrow would be a better day, she hoped. And, whatever happened, at least she wouldn't have to answer to an angry Adam Dalton about it.

Chapter Two

"So you came to the Open House. Heather said you might," a vaguely familiar voice commented. Angela stood up from adjusting her shoe to come face-to-face with Adam Dalton for the second time in one week. Only, this time he looked much friendlier—more like the man she remembered from the pool.

"Hello, Mr. Dalton," she responded. "My kids wanted me to attend this function tonight. They enjoy the recreation center very much. And they have friends here they wanted to see." She had been aware of the inevitability of running into him here, but she hadn't thought he would look quite this appealing. Dark brown slacks, cream-colored shirt and a tie swirled with coordinating colors—all suited him well. As did the smile he offered, in place of the glare she remembered.

"Please, call me 'Adam,'" he said quietly. "I'm glad you're here. I owe you an apology."

"No, you don't. You helped Heather out of what could have been a serious situation, and I appreciate that. I'm sorry if I was rude when you brought her home."

"No, really, you weren't. I was. I would never have made such a harsh remark about you and your husband...if I had realized the situation. I apologize for my comment." He had regretted his thoughtless statement from the moment that he had learned of Angela's recent loss.

Angela knew that he felt badly about his sharp words. She could see it in his eyes. "Apology accepted," she said. "No harm done."

"Good," he replied, as a seriousness darkened his expression. "I didn't know then that Heather's father had died."

"Yes, well, I suppose it's unlikely you would have known. Heather doesn't talk much about her dad."

Adam nodded, and they stood in awkward silence for a moment. "I'm sure it's been difficult."

"It's been very hard on the kids. They were still trying to adjust to the idea of a divorce when Dan was killed, so it's not been easy."

"I didn't realize you were divorced."

"We were in the process...which gives me a rather unusual status. I'm not quite divorced, but I'm not really a widow, either. I haven't figured it all out yet."

One corner of Adam's mouth curved upward in a

brief acknowledging smile. "I've been in situations I haven't been able to figure out, too. It's not a comfortable place to be."

"No, it's not," she agreed with a small smile. "So, maybe we should change the subject. Can you tell me about swimming lessons? How is Heather doing?"

"Well, she's doing fine—basically—but I'm concerned about her not moving up to the next class."

"She's been stuck at this level too long, hasn't she?"

Adam shrugged. "I don't have a problem with children repeating lessons. That's necessary sometimes. But Heather really needs only one thing more before she can move on."

Angela nodded. "The dive."

"Exactly," Adam agreed. "She needs to go off the board into twelve feet of water. There will be an instructor in the pool waiting for her, but she just doesn't want to do it."

"That's odd. She hasn't said anything about it this time. During the summer session she was very anxious about that part. Then she decided she wasn't ready to dive and just didn't do it. I told her that was fine...to wait until she felt ready," Angela explained and glanced around the reception area until she glimpsed her daughter.

"And it's basically the same situation this fall," said Adam. "I know she can do this. I think even *she* knows she can, too...but she won't. And she'll only get another certificate of participation instead of the certificate of completion she needs to go on. If she repeats this level again, she'll be the oldest kid in the group, and I'm worried about what that will do to her self-esteem, Mrs. Sanders—''

''My name is Angela,'' she corrected. ''And I'll speak to Heather about it again and encourage her, but I won't tell her she has to dive. The whole learning-to-swim issue has been difficult enough.''

''She didn't want to learn?'' Adam asked.

''Not really. We finally talked her into it, but she was very 'iffy' about the idea.''

''Are you afraid of water, Angela?''

''No, I wouldn't say I'm afraid of it, but I'm not a swimmer either, so I have a healthy respect for it.''

Adam smiled and looked over at some children playing by the front door. ''So that's where Heather's fear comes from.'' Then his gaze returned to Angela's face. This woman didn't look as if she'd be afraid of anything. No, she seemed determined, set in her ways possibly. And she looked far more attractive in this stylish green suit than she had in a sweat suit.

''As a parent, I'd prefer to be thought of in some way other than the source of my child's fears,'' Angela stated bluntly. She looked straight into the charcoal-gray eyes that seemed to be amused by her—although his grin had faded.

''I wasn't being critical. Just logical. Lots of kids' insecurities can be traced back to the things their mothers are afraid of.''

''Or fathers, I would assume?'' she added.

''Or fathers,'' he agreed. ''I stand corrected.'' He knew they needed a change in conversation. ''So, have you and your children used the rec center much over the years?" he asked, sliding one hand into the pocket of his dark slacks. "I've only been here about a year. I'm not really familiar with who the long-standing members are."

"Heather has taken a number of classes here. My two sons also come occasionally."

"Two? I thought Nathan was Heather's only brother. I remember him from the summer session. He took karate, didn't he?"

"Yes, and there's David, too. He's more into studying than anything right now. He wants to earn a college scholarship so he can go to law school and make a lot of money like his Uncle Rob used to do."

"Used to do? Why? What happened to Uncle Rob?" Adam asked in sudden curiosity.

"He left the legal profession to enter the ministry." Angela smiled. "I've never seen him happier."

"The change agrees with him that much?"

"It probably feels good to stop running from God. He spent about a decade doing that. And it also helps that he now has the wife of his dreams and twins on the way."

"The twins may be a bigger adjustment than the loss of income was," Adam remarked, his eyes twinkling.

"Rob's always been good with kids. Mine, especially. He'll do fine."

Adam nodded. "When it comes to dealing with children, you're either good at it or you're not. There's not much gray area there, in my opinion. At least, that's been my experience over the years—both at work and in real life.''

Angela was curious about his comment, but didn't want to pry. ''You work around kids here all day long. You must be very good with them.''

''Not having any of my own probably makes it easier to be with them so much here at the center.''

''You don't have any of your own?'' Angela repeated, surprised. He certainly looked like the family type.

Adam didn't answer immediately, which puzzled Angela.

''No,'' he said after a moment's hesitation. ''The only family I have is my brother, his wife and their daughter.'' Abruptly, he looked toward the refreshment table. ''Could I get you some coffee?''

''I'd like that,'' she responded, and watched him leave to get their drinks. She glanced around the room to check on Heather, Nathan and David, all of whom she caught sight of over by the bleachers talking with friends.

Then Adam returned. She smiled as she accepted the foam cup. ''Thanks.''

''It's black. I didn't know—''

''That's fine...really,'' she answered a little nervously. She would never have guessed that it would be so awkward—and yet so pleasant—to share a conversation with this man. She almost wished that it wasn't pleasant.

''So...what do you think about Heather?'' Adam continued, obviously not intending to return to the subject of his life. "Would you be willing to talk to her about going off the board? This session ends in mid-November. That's not a lot of time."

"I'll discuss it with her. I'd like to see her advance in the series."

"She could probably be on the swim team if she wanted to try," Adam added.

Angela shook her head. "I don't think she'd do that. She's not as competitive as her brothers. Team sports haven't interested her at all."

"It was just a thought. You know, if you could come to a lesson or two and watch her, it might be just the encouragement she needs."

"I'll try. It's difficult sometimes with my schedule to do little things like that, although I know it would mean a lot to her." A familiar pang of guilt tugged at Angela. How would she ever have the time to do all the little things that would mean a lot to her kids?

"Where do you work?"

"I'm principal of a private Christian school on the west side of town. This is my first year at it, and I spend too much time there. I taught for so many years and now that seems almost easy compared to this job."

"I was a teacher, too," Adam remarked, watching some other parents and visitors enter the lobby. "Algebra...geometry..."

"Math? I'm envious. That was never my strong point. I taught primary grades. First grade for several years, then second for five more before I moved into administration." She shivered slightly, appreciating the warmth of the cup in her hands. The cool night air of autumn blew in through the center's heavy front doors that opened and closed as visitors came and went.

"There." Adam, obviously noticing her shiver, pointed to an empty space near the drinking fountain. "You'll be warmer over by that wall."

When she turned to move, he cupped her elbow with his hand directing her to the spot that he had indicated. Angela was suddenly aware—too aware—of his momentary touch and it startled her.

"So we both left teaching for administrative jobs," Adam remarked, taking a drink of his coffee. "Any regrets?"

"Regrets?" Angela thought for a moment. "I guess I have about a thousand of them, but none have to do with leaving teaching. I needed to make a change, and I needed more income, so...it's a challenge, but one I enjoy."

He nodded in recognition of her answer. "Me, too," he agreed. "Teaching was great for a while, but I was ready to do something different. Then this job at the center came up. It seemed like the perfect solution."

"Is it?" she asked.

"For now," Adam responded. She saw him surveying the lobby, now filled with all age groups—from preschoolers to some senior citizens. "I suppose I should be mingling with the visitors, although that's my least favorite part of this job."

"Adam!" They both turned at the sudden sound of his name.

"Adam," a young woman at his elbow repeated emphatically. "There are other people here you should meet," she insisted with her brow creased in disapproval.

She was a beautiful young woman, Angela noticed, no more than college age, she estimated—at least a decade younger than Angela or Adam. She had gorgeous curly black hair and wore a short navy blue skirt and a sweater of deep red.

Adam nodded in acknowledgment. "Excuse me," he said to Angela. "That's my assistant."

"Your assistant?" she commented quietly, offering a wry smile.

Adam frowned and glanced again at the woman who was already slipping back into the crowd of visitors. Then he returned his gaze to Angela. "Yes, well..." he began as an easy smile played at the corners of his mouth. "She's very—"

"Young?" Angela finished.

And Adam chuckled quietly, tiny laugh lines crinkling around his eyes. "Yes, so she is. However, she's also right. I *should* be mingling with the crowd since I'm the director."

"True," Angela said politely, and nodded toward the attractive associate. "You'd better go to...."

"Tiffany," Adam responded, his gray eyes flashing with humor and a mischievous grin curving his mouth. He paused. "Actually, Tiffany is my brother's stepdaughter. So...she's my niece...."

"...sort of?" Angela offered.

Adam shook his head. "She's as intelligent as she is attractive. And she's engaged to the coach of the swim team."

Engaged. Angela wondered how that felt. The thought made her feel even older than the lovely, raven-haired niece had managed to do. Engaged was an experience she'd never known. First, she'd been a college kid, living in a dorm. Then she was married and a mother—almost overnight, it seemed. And now, at 32, a parent of three—and widowed. Or almost divorced. Or whatever. Where had the years gone?

"Oh, to be young again," she said more wistfully than she'd intended. She looked from Tiffany to Adam's suddenly serious expression.

"Youth isn't everything," he remarked, seeming to sense the trace of heartache in her tone. "There's a lot to be said for the wisdom that comes with the years."

"Let's hope so," she replied. "I'd like to think something gets better with time." She raised her cup. "Thanks for the coffee."

He nodded. "You're welcome. Are you free this Thursday to come to Heather's lesson?"

"I'll check my schedule," she answered and then nervously cleared her throat. Suddenly she felt the need to find some conflict on her calendar. She'd seen enough of Adam Dalton for one week. The very last thing she needed was interest—however remote—in a man. Even if he did have the warmest eyes she'd ever seen.

"I've enjoyed talking with you," he commented quietly. "Very much."

The first part was an obligatory remark, Angela knew. The last part was not. She nodded her head slightly before acknowledging. "Me, too."

"Maybe I'll see you Thursday," he said before excusing himself to join Tiffany and fulfill his role as the director.

Angela drank the last of her coffee, dropped the empty cup into the trash receptacle beside the door, and went in search of her children.

Heather saw her mother approaching and came to meet her. "We've been having fun, Mom. The boys are over here talking about video games." She clasped Angela's hand and led her to where Nathan and David sat, eating popcorn and talking with other youngsters.

"Time to go, gang. We've got things to do," she announced. After some stalling, her children had found their jackets, said goodbye to friends and were on their way out the front door.

Against her better judgment, Angela did not resist glancing back into the thinning crowd to the spot where she'd last seen Adam speaking with an older gentleman. And he stood there still, listening to whatever the man was saying. But, to Angela's surprise, his gaze returned to her at that moment.

She wasn't sure who smiled first, but she hoped it was him. Otherwise, she was openly flirting, and she hadn't meant to do that. What would come next? she wondered miserably. She saw Adam give a slight nod of farewell before she returned her attention to the matter at hand—getting three children home.

Later that evening, all homework done, prayers said and children asleep, Angela finally sank into the comfort of her own bed. And that's when her thoughts returned to Adam just as surely as his gaze had returned to hers when she was leaving the center.

"Lord, I'm too old for a silly schoolgirl crush and too new at this sort of thing to know how I should feel. I'm not ready for an Adam Dalton in my life. Let someone else have him." She murmured the words before the sleep she needed finally came.

But Adam was not quite as quick to turn his back on new feelings. It had been such a long time since he'd felt this pang of interest in anyone, and he was relieved to know that he was still capable of it. Angela Sanders. She was pretty, independent, strong but still a little unsure of herself at times. And her eyes.... Adam poured himself a cup of decaf and walked toward the window, where he stood staring out at the few stars shining in the September darkness. Those eyes of light blue were filled with a tenderness he'd not seen before tonight. Intelligence, humor, vulnerability, caution—all that and more lay in those depths, he felt certain. Suddenly, Adam wanted to know all the thoughts behind those eyes and the soft angular lines of Angela's lovely face.

It had actually been difficult to walk away from her this evening. There was a sense of familiarity with her that far exceeded any earned by their brief and unpleasant encounter the night he'd taken Heather home. It was more than that, more than anything he could explain. He wondered, for the first time in years...if he made the effort to get to know this woman better...if he gained her trust, however long it took...would she be willing to accept him for what he was—just the way the Lord had done years earlier?

Chapter Three

Thursday came quickly. As the afternoon hours advanced to evening, Angela weighed her excuses to miss Heather's swimming lessons—and avoid Adam Dalton—against her daughter's need for support and encouragement.

"Oh, all right, I give up." She spoke aloud to herself as she gathered up her coat and purse and shut off the lights in her office. "I'll go. I dread seeing Adam Dalton, but Heather needs me. I'll go."

And Heather was delighted. After eating a quick dinner at the children's favorite fast-food restaurant, Angela dropped the boys and their homework at her parents' house. Then she and Heather headed for the recreation center.

Soon Heather had changed into her hot-pink swimsuit, and Angela had looked over her own dusty pink skirt and jacket and ivory blouse in the mirror in the women's locker room. They looked a little wrinkled and weary from the day—both she *and* the clothes, Angela mused. But maybe that was a good thing. She didn't need any further interest from Adam Dalton, and he surely wouldn't take notice of her—not looking like this. And not with all the young female employees in and out of the center daily. And maybe he hadn't had any interest in her in the first place. Maybe it had all just been her imagination. But still, the way he had looked back at her as she was leaving the Open House that night....

"Mom! Let's go!" Heather exclaimed, cutting into her mother's thoughts. She draped a towel around her bare shoulders.

They hurried to the pool area, and Heather quickly joined her group of a dozen or so boys and girls at the shallow end. Angela turned to take a seat in the nearby bleachers to watch the two young women who were coordinating the class as they began working with the children.

Angela glanced around briefly and saw no sign of Adam. That was good, she thought. Easy. Simple. And she must have been wrong about his interest in her. After all, he hadn't said that he would definitely be here on Thursday for Heather's lesson. She'd assumed more than she should have and, she thought with a sigh, it certainly hadn't been the first time in life she'd made that mistake.

Angela leaned back against the bleachers and enjoyed her daughter's antics in the water. Heather was swimming very well, just as Angela knew her girl could do—*if* she wanted to. But getting Heather to "want to" had been the struggle all along. Angela waved when Heather looked up a couple of times for Mom's approval. It certainly appeared to Angela that Heather was more than ready to move on to the higher level with the rest of her class. She followed every request of either instructor without problem or hesitation.

The door opened at the side of the pool, and Angela looked over her shoulder to find Adam walking toward her. He smiled before he spoke.

"I'm glad you could come. You've been watching her?" He sat down beside Angela.

"Yes. She seems to be doing everything they ask," Angela remarked, turning her attention to her little girl.

Adam nodded his head. "She can do everything needed to complete this level—including the dive. But she needs more confidence...maybe some more encouragement."

Angela agreed. "I'll talk to her again, but I won't force her to dive. She has to want to do it herself."

"Fair enough," Adam commented. "But maybe if she believed in her abilities a little more strongly, she would want to try."

"Maybe. You did say someone would be there in the water waiting for her, right?" Angela asked.

"Yes, there's nothing to be afraid of," he assured her.

"Maybe she needs to trust her instructors more. I'll ask her. Maybe that's what's holding her back."

"Maybe you're right. Could be she doesn't have enough confidence in the instructors."

Angela smiled. Heather was too much like her. "Trusting people doesn't come easily to her."

"Did she learn that from her mother, too?" Adam asked quietly, the warmth in his eyes never wavering. A warmth she'd never seen in Dan's gaze.

But Angela looked away without answering. Uneasiness settled over her. It had been a long time since she'd really trusted anyone except family members. And she hadn't planned to allow herself to be in such a vulnerable position again. Ever.

"Mom!" Heather climbed out of the pool and reached for her towel.

"Hi, hon!" Angela waved. "I'll be right there." She glanced back at Adam to say goodbye, only to find him looking over at her daughter.

"Good job, Heather." He stood up, walking with Angela around to the other side of the pool where Heather was drying her face and hair with a beach towel. "Would you and your mom like to go out for some ice cream?" Adam asked the young swimmer.

Heather's face lit up, just as Angela frowned.

"That would be great!" the child responded. "Can we, Mom? It's not very late and I don't have any homework to do when we get home."

Angela looked from Heather's bright eyes to Adam, who stood studying her thoughtfully.

"Think you can trust me enough for that?" he inquired with a half smile. He was not at all certain she'd agree.

"Do I have a choice?" she countered as Heather wrapped her arms tightly around Angela's waist.

"Can we, Mom? Please?"

"I guess we could go for a little while," Angela replied. She regarded Adam's expression of satisfaction with irritation. "You cheated."

"Next time, I won't need to," he responded, and reached for Heather's hand as they headed toward the door. "I want to lock up my office. When Heather is changed, meet me at the front door."

"See you in a minute," Heather said, pulling free from Adam's grasp and running into the locker room.

"All right?" He tilted his head to the side, awaiting Angela's reply.

She nodded. "See you in a minute," she echoed her daughter's comment. "Ready or not."

"I'll be ready," he responded, then disappeared through the door to his office.

But would *she* ever be ready to have another man in her life after living through twelve years of the mistake she'd made in marrying Dan Sanders? Was her judgment of men good enough that she'd ever take another chance with one? "No," she reminded herself, "no, no, no." She wouldn't risk making the same error again, wouldn't even come close to it...or to any man who might interest her enough to threaten her freedom. No one could be worth that. Not even this guy.

Heather dried her hair quickly and changed into her jeans and a T-shirt. "Mom, I'm ready. Let's go!" she said, motioning Angela toward the door. "Adam's waiting."

"Yes, he is," Angela sighed, and they headed for the lobby.

"Mint chocolate chip." Heather gave her order to Adam. "Two scoops. It's my favorite."

"And what is your mom's favorite?" Adam asked Heather, but looked over at Angela for a reply.

"A small chocolate milk shake would be great," Angela said immediately, hoping to squelch Heather's probable response.

"But Mom, you *always* have that big caramel sundae with the peanuts and all that whipped cr—" Angela's hand moved deftly to cover her daughter's open mouth—a move it had made numerous times in six years. She caught the smile of amusement on Adam's face. Angela had eaten only one sundae like that in the past six months, but Heather made it sound as though it was a part of her daily diet. She started to explain, but suddenly it was their turn at the counter.

"Mint chocolate chip, double-scoop cone and two large caramel sundaes with nuts and whipped cream," Adam requested.

"The milk shake would have been fine," she said, and released her hold on her child.

Adam's laugh was gentle. "There's no need to settle for 'fine.' This will be better."

"That's true," she admitted, her mouth curving into a reluctant smile. Oh, well, she knew she'd never have a figure like Tiffany's. Not even if she gave up eating altogether.

Soon they were seated at a table, enjoying the desserts. Conversation flowed between Adam and Angela, more easily than it had at the Open House. They discussed some activities at the center, and Angela's job as principal. Heather added some thoughts of her own along the way. Then the youngster had a serious question for Adam.

"Are you a Christian?" They were the blunt words of a six-year-old.

Angela cringed. She would have asked him, too, but not quite so openly or loudly.

"Yes," Adam answered easily, "I go to First Church on Third Avenue."

"That's where my sister-in-law attended before she and Rob moved away," Angela said, suddenly distracted from Heather's tactlessness.

"Lots of people go to church," Heather continued. "But I mean are you really a Christian?"

"Yes, I accepted Christ into my heart over seven years ago," he explained to Heather before turning his attention back to Angela. "You mean Rob, the lawyer turned minister? *His* wife?"

"Yes, Micah Granston. Shepherd was her last name before she married my brother. Do you remember her? She had very long reddish hair then. It's much shorter now. She's a teacher and an artist."

"I've only been going there since I moved to this area about a year and a half ago. She may have left before I joined that church. How long have they been married?''

''About two years. A little more than that, actually,'' Angela said. ''So she would have been gone by the time you started there. But she always liked that church.''

''I do, too. It's just what I was looking for,'' Adam added. ''Where do you attend?''

''Mount Pleasant on Oakwood Avenue,'' Heather answered for her mother. ''We're Christians, too, you know.''

''I know,'' he answered.

''How?'' Heather asked, a frown scrunching up her freckled face. ''How could you know without asking?''

''I guess...,'' he began, ''it's just something I sensed.'' His eyes rose to meet Angela's and, for a long moment, held them. She couldn't remember a look feeling any more intense than the heart-stopping gaze she now shared with Adam. Did he feel it, too?

But interruption came swiftly. Heather had more ground to cover. ''My brothers are Christians, too, and Grandma and Grandpa, and so are Uncle Rob and Aunt Micah and Uncle Eric and—''

''I think he gets the picture, hon,'' Angela interjected before glancing back at her daughter. ''Heather may become the next preacher in the family.''

''She'd be good at it,'' Adam said. ''She could have a lot of converts under her direct style of witnessing.''

''Right, she'll either have a lot or know the reason

why not,'' Angela replied with a laugh. She allowed herself to study Adam's face. Touches of humor lingered around his mouth and eyes, but something about the set of his jaw made him, at times, she thought, look rather stubborn.

''Are your mother and father Christians, too?'' Heather continued her quest for knowledge. She had inherited that quality from her grandfather, the snoopy one in the family, Angela thought with relief. There's at least one flaw she hadn't directly inflicted on her offspring. It was one generation removed.

''No, my parents weren't saved. They weren't interested in religion of any kind,'' Adam stated. ''In fact, I can't remember being in a church with them for anything other than a wedding or two.'' He glanced at Heather's suddenly startled expression.

''Wow!'' she exclaimed. ''That must have felt weird. I mean, what did you do on Sunday mornings and Sunday nights?''

''We slept late in the mornings, and on Sunday evenings we...probably watched a lot of television if it was bad weather, and played outdoors if it was nice. It seems like such a long time ago,'' he added.

Living under their parents' roof had happened a long time ago for both of them, Angela thought. His eyes met hers again with a contemplative look, and she wondered about the thoughts behind it.

''And they still don't go to church?'' Heather persisted.

Adam shook his head without looking away from Angela's steady blue gaze. ''They've both died. My father had a heart attack when he was only fifty-four."

"So young?" Angela asked.

"That's not young," Heather informed them. "Mom, you know Grandpa is fifty-four!"

Adam and Angela both laughed a little. Then Adam offered, "I guess it depends on your perspective."

Their perspectives both came from the thirty-something bracket. Angela guessed probably thirty-four or thirty-five for Adam as she glanced at his dark blond hair, cut short and tapered neatly to the collar of his plaid shirt. She particularly liked the crinkly laugh lines at the corners of his eyes when he smiled. That gave him a friendly, appealing look that Angela was certain she wasn't the first female to notice.

She realized Adam was assessing her, too, from across the table, and wished for a moment that she could read his mind. Then she decided that it was probably better that she couldn't. She might be disappointed. However, in the smokey gray of his eyes, she saw what she was sure was a gleam of interest.

Eventually they finished their ice cream and made the short walk to Adam's silver pickup truck for the ride back to the center. Heather climbed into the middle of the front seat; Angela joined her on the passenger side, and Adam shut the door. Then he drove back to the large parking lot where he pulled the truck up next to Angela's very used, dark green van. The wear and tear of three kids and their friends over the years had a way of aging anything. Including moms.

Heather hopped from the truck to her seat in the

van, and Angela and Adam walked across to the driver's door.

"How was your ice cream?" he asked as they lingered a moment.

"Never better," she answered honestly. And it had little to do with the caramel or the peanuts, she thought.

"My thoughts exactly." Adam smiled, but a sudden seriousness stole over his expression. Angela lowered her eyes to look at his hand where it rested on the door handle. But the door remained closed. "Will you go to dinner with me sometime? We'll take the kids with us."

"I don't know, Adam," she said cautiously. "It's been a long time...I'm not very good at this sort of thing." She didn't glance up. She didn't need the encouragement of a tender look.

"Oh, I don't know about that. I think you handled that sundae about as well as any other woman I've been out with in the last few years." He opened her door, and she got into the driver's seat—which, she thought ironically, was exactly where she was in the relationship. It could go forward...or die right here and now in this parking lot. It was her call.

"Your kids can even pick the restaurant," he offered, "as long as it's something other than fast food."

Sure, Angela argued with herself, she liked him, but she could be wrong about him the same as she'd been wrong about Dan. She didn't want another "unhappily ever after" relationship. Solitude—even loneliness—sounded better than that. But turning him down now might make him more determined to win her over. Maybe she could make a date with him to show him how wrong it could be for them. What could she invite him to do that would discourage any interest that had been kindled? Then she remembered the church cookout.

"Why don't you go to dinner with us?" she asked with a smile. "There's a church cookout a week from Saturday that starts in the afternoon and lasts until dark. The kids and I are going. So are Mom and Dad. It's for the church family and their guests." Most of whom Adam couldn't know—certainly a daunting enough invitation for a man.

Adam looked away from her for a moment. Then he looked back into her eyes. "What time should I pick you up?"

Angela blinked. She hadn't even thought that far ahead. "I guess...around three...would be good."

The door to the van closed securely. "I'll see you then," he stated. "Be careful driving home. 'Bye, Heather." He paused. "Angela, I'm glad you went with me tonight. I know this is...awkward for you."

She nodded and smiled. He understood her better than she wanted him to. Then she said good-night, and drove away, exhaling a deep sigh.

"What's wrong, Mom? Didn't you have a good time?" Heather asked.

Angela felt her daughter studying her frowning profile. "I don't know enough about Adam Dalton to have as good a time with him as I did."

"How can you ever get to know him if you don't spend time with him? He's a really nice man. You'll see."

But Angela had already seen...and she was beginning to feel, too. That was the part she hadn't expected. He seemed kind. Overall, he appeared to be one of the new "sensitive" type of men she'd seen over the years but had not experienced for herself. She thought briefly of her brothers: Rob and Eric were both better husbands than any she knew—including her own father. Now, here was Adam. Was he really the way he appeared to be and, if so, why hadn't he already met the right woman and settled down with a family? Why would he want to consider being involved in her life...with her children? And why couldn't she just send him away instead of playing with fire?

"Why don't you like him?" Heather persisted.

"I do like him, Heather," Angela said. "But I don't know if I want to date him...have a relationship with him. Do you understand what I mean?"

"You mean like be his girlfriend?"

"Exactly. I don't think I want to do anything like that right now. I don't think I'm ready for that."

"You are getting older all the time, Mom. When do you think you might be ready for that?"

Angela laughed more from surprise than from amusement. "So I'm getting older. That doesn't mean I need to rush to find a husband so I'll have someone to grow old with. Being alone would be better than being with the wrong person."

And how can I know? she asked inwardly. *Lord, how can I be sure seeing Adam is a wise choice? I can't endure another mistake. Not now—not with the kids to consider.* Still she couldn't deny the feeling that stirred deep inside when their eyes had met in a lingering gaze.

"How do you know Adam is the wrong person for you?" Heather asked.

"How do you know he's *not?*" Angela countered.

"He has friendly eyes."

"Eyes?" Angela repeated. "You noticed that, too?"

"Sure. Maybe we have friendly eyes, too. Maybe that's what made him think we were Christians before he knew for sure. You think so, Mom?"

Angela smiled and reached over to squeeze Heather's left hand. "Could be, honey. I've not really thought about that before." There were lots of things she'd not considered before now. Like wanting another man in her life…like imagining that man might be Adam.

More than a week passed before the cookout, and they were days filled with life—the dailiness of it—school, work, housecleaning, cooking, laundry, church attendance, appointments, nightly homework. Then Thursday-night swimming came around again.

Heather remained reluctant to dive despite her mother's encouragement, and Angela couldn't go to lessons with her due to a meeting at the school. When she picked up Heather at the center that evening,

Adam was not around. Much later that evening, long after the kids were in bed, Angela sat down in the quietness of her kitchen with a cup of tea. She hoped Adam wouldn't forget about Saturday. And then, she hoped that he would. If he was going to hurt Heather's feelings, or anyone else's, she'd rather it happened now—early in the game.

The phone rang, startling Angela in the near darkness of the room. Maybe it was Adam calling to cancel. Or to confirm. She picked up the receiver, but the voice on the other end of the line was the soft voice of a friend.

"Micah! I haven't talked to you for days! How are you?"

"Tired. And fat. You can't believe the weight I've gained," Micah answered. "I had never thought of myself as vain but now, all of a sudden, I can't stand to walk past a mirror."

"You're having twins. You can't expect to weigh your usual amount—which is…what? About 100 pounds at most?"

"No, more like 120, but I can't believe the numbers on the scales—numbers Rob has to read to me because I can't see past my belly," Micah complained with a sigh.

"Micah—"

"I know, I know. This is a lesson in self-pity. You'll have to forgive me. I'm in the everything-makes-me-want-to-cry stage."

"I've been there. Three times, remember?" Angela said gently. "Don't be so hard on yourself. At least you've got a good reason for your clothes to feel snug. I'm sitting here, trying to figure out how to drop five pounds by Saturday so I can find something in my closet to wear for a date.''

''A date? That's fantastic,'' Micah replied. ''With who?''

''Just some man I met. I'm sorry now I ever agreed to it.'' Angela lamented. ''How could I be so foolish? I have kids, a new job to learn, rent to pay—''

''What's his name?'' Micah cut short Angela's list of responsibilities. ''Where did you meet him?''

''It's kind of a long story, but his name is Adam Dalton. He's the director at the recreation center where Heather takes swimming lessons.'' Angela sighed, almost relieved to actually be saying aloud the thoughts that had been running through her mind. ''He's...different. Kind, funny, good-looking, interesting...and, apparently, interested.''

''Hmm, all of those qualities rolled up into one package? I thought I'd grabbed the only one of those on the market.''

''No, there's at least one more, and he's just what I *don't* need.''

Micah laughed. ''Don't be so pessimistic. This could be the guy for you. Hold on a second.''

Angela listened to Micah talking to her husband and to what she could hear of Rob's voice in the background. She knew he'd have something to say on the subject—once he knew the subject existed.

''Angela's met somebody...of course, I mean a man...yes, I'll ask her.'' Micah directed her voice into the phone again. "Angela, Rob wants to know—"

"Tell my brother that Adam is a Christian, has been for seven years and attends First Church where you used to go."

Micah relayed the message to Rob before apologizing to Angela. "He's just concerned about you, you know that."

"Well, I'm concerned about me, too. And I'm not a naive college student about to make another blunder with my life, if that's what he thinks," Angela said.

"Listen, Rob loves you and you love him. And I'm not foolish enough to get caught in the middle of a sibling quarrel. You can talk to him about this later. Right now, I want you to forget you're my sister-in-law. Just be my friend and tell me about this great guy."

"I don't know, Micah. He makes me wish I were younger...prettier—"

"So this *could* be serious then," Micah commented. "Have you gone out with him yet? I mean, been alone with him?"

"Yes. No. We went out one evening for ice cream. Heather was with us," Angela explained.

"You are going out with him again, aren't you? I mean, Rob and I could watch the kids—" Micah stopped. "Hold on, Angela.... Rob, you'll have to tell her that yourself. You can talk to her as soon as I'm finished. Sorry, Angela. Anyway, as I was saying, we'll watch the kids for you."

"He's going to a church cookout with us on Saturday. I don't need a sitter for that. And tell Rob that the kids, Mom and Dad, and about 200 other church members will be there to chaperone."

"Not exactly a romantic setting," Micah replied. "But it might be a good way to get to know him better. When I first met Rob...well, I remember wanting to kiss him long before we actually did. And once that happened, then I knew."

Angela waited. "You knew...what?"

"That I would want to be with him forever," Micah said with a sigh and then a gentle laugh. "Angela, I think I'm supposed to hang up now. My husband is...making funny faces...." Micah laughed. "Rob, stop it—"

"All right, you two. Call me tomorrow. 'Bye." Angela hung up the receiver and walked into the darkened living room. She sank wearily onto the sofa. The kids were asleep. The house was quiet. And she'd never been in love the way Rob and Micah were. Or Eric and Hope. Or even her own mother and father. She was genuinely glad for the happy marriages in the Granston family, and, at the same time, so jealous that she could almost have cried.

Chapter Four

Three o'clock loomed near that Saturday afternoon, and Angela looked at her reflection in the full-length mirror hanging on the back of her bathroom door. Her jeans were rather old and faded—just the way she liked them. And her white shirt and colorful vest looked acceptable, she thought as she viewed the patchwork of rich browns, rusts and tans. She pulled on her saddle-colored boots and frowned. Acceptable, yes; attractive, not particularly. But her dark hair looked good with its new layered cut, and her bangs weren't too long or too short for a change, so that pleased her. What difference did it really make anyway? It was just a church outing—and probably the only date she'd ever have with Adam Dalton.

"Mom, I've put the cooler and the basket in the back of the van. Are you almost ready?" Nathan called to her from the living room. "David and

Heather are goofing around out back. Should I tell them it's time to go?''

''No, wait until Adam gets here.''

''Maybe he won't show,'' Nathan offered with a hopeful smile when he appeared in the bathroom doorway.

Angela shot a look of obvious irritation in the direction of her son before walking past him to find the sweater she wanted to take along. ''Maybe he won't,'' she agreed, ''but maybe he will. Either way, you're still going to this cookout. Tell your brother and sister to get their jackets. You'll all need them before this is over.''

Nathan was not enthusiastic over this new development in her life—in *all* their lives, Angela reminded herself. Everything she did affected the kids one way or another, and her involvement with Adam was no different. That's why this relationship would probably go no further than sharing a hamburger with him today in the presence of her children, her parents and dozens of other people. People, people everywhere. Why had she invited him to this gathering, anyway? What was she thinking? They'd spend hours together in a crowd when all she really wanted was five minutes alone with him.

Unable to locate her sweater, she pulled a corduroy jacket from where she'd left it on the corner of her dresser and paused to look one last time into a small mirror that hung on her bedroom wall. *Five minutes alone with him?* Where had that thought come from? she wondered suddenly. Then she remembered Micah's comment about wanting to kiss Rob. But it had been years since Angela had felt that way—so many, in fact that she couldn't clearly remember *ever* having had that feeling. And now, to feel this way about a man she hadn't heard from in a week and a half, a man who might not even remember he made this date with her, a man who might not be any more reliable than her husband had been....

Then the doorbell rang. Angela breathed a sigh of relief; Nathan groaned quietly, then went to answer the door. Maybe Adam was different, she thought. The possibility existed, didn't it? Otherwise, what was the point in trying?

"Hi, Nathan." She heard Adam's familiar voice greet her less-than-enthusiastic son. This would be trying for Nathan. There was no doubt about that. He was a sensitive kid who had taken the idea of being "man of the house" too seriously, for too long. He'd seen more clearly than his siblings the effect his father's problem with alcohol had had on the family, and he'd probably be suspicious of any possible intrusion on their now-pleasant home life. For that matter, so was Angela. So what was she going to do about this man standing in the middle of her living room?

"Hi," she said as she came forward to greet Adam. "Ready for a cookout?" She thought she detected a slight ready-as-I'll-ever-be set to his expression.

"Guess so. Want me to carry anything to the van?"

"I already took care of that," Nathan interjected and grabbed his school jacket from a hook by the door. "I'll tell the others it's time to go." He exited without further comment.

They both watched him go; then Adam looked back at Angela. "This is difficult for him," he commented.

She nodded. "He'll feel better once we're there and he sees his friends," she replied.

There was silence between them for an awkward moment. Then Adam spoke. "I brought a case of soda and put it in your van. I thought I should contribute something to this outing."

"The kids will like it. I'm taking potato salad, baked beans and some cookies I bought at the bakery. Mom is bringing a cake, a relish tray and iced tea. I'm sure we'll have plenty of everything. We always do," she explained with a smile. "If there's anything our church excels at, it's carry-in dinners. We like to eat."

Adam grinned. "You've changed your hair."

"Just a little," she said, thinking how much she liked his easy smile. "It was overdue for a cut, and I can't stand my bangs down around my eyes." She reached for her car keys on the nearby end table and, amazingly for a change, they were actually where she'd left them.

"It looks good," Adam complimented as he opened the door for her, realizing the remark about her hair seemed lackluster, but he couldn't tell her how pretty he thought she was. In jeans and a plain shirt, in a skirt and a jacket, in whatever she chose to wear. That might be too much too soon. It would be the absolute truth, but she probably wouldn't believe him. And he needed her to believe him. Now, and later. "You look great every time I see you."

Angela cocked her head to the side, eyeing him with skepticism. "Especially with a runny nose and wearing that old sweat suit I had on the first night we spoke."

"Yes, well—" he remembered that encounter with clarity "— you looked very...."

"Very?" she said, knowing he was struggling for a descriptive, but safe, word. "I'm waiting."

"I'm thinking," Adam replied with a smile. "Can I say 'motherly'? 'Cautious'? 'Protective' maybe?"

"Nope," she answered as she walked toward and then past him. "You could say 'awful.'" He was close enough to touch, and Angela was fighting the urge to do exactly that when Adam extended an arm, clasping her hand warmly in his own.

"How about 'cute'?" he suggested.

"Sorry, but 'cute' is not acceptable at thirty-two," she replied, holding tightly to the strong hand she had welcomed.

"Then let's go with 'promising,'" he said, with a gentle squeeze to her fingers.

Promising. What a lovely thought. But she didn't dare say that. Not to this man she knew so little about. "I wasn't sure you'd come today," she admitted suddenly.

"Why?" he asked, studying the contemplative blue of her eyes. "I told you I'd be here at three."

"I know, but..." How could she tell him the reasons behind her doubts? Did she really want to explain the years with Dan?

"You can't tell me you've had that happen with many dates before. Being stood up," he added as they stepped outside into the sunshine and made their way toward the van. The children were already climbing in.

No, she thought, the problem had never been with a date. It was only when matrimony entered the story line that keeping commitments had become an issue. Marriage and responsibility had not sat well with her husband, and she had grown to expect broken promises. "I guess I'm just pessimistic by nature." And experience.

"Maybe that can be changed," he suggested.

Maybe it could, but at this point in her life, Angela had her doubts.

"Is the truck okay parked off to the side like that?" Adam asked. "I knew we'd need to take your van."

She raised her hand to shield her eyes from the afternoon sun. "That's fine." Then she held up her keys. "But would you mind doing the driving?"

He opened the passenger door for her. "Not at all." He let go of her hand, and she climbed in.

"You ready, kids?" she asked, glancing back at two excited faces—and Nathan's frown.

"It's about a mile farther down this road. Then make the next left." They were nearing their destination as Heather asked for the third time how long this trip would last.

"Just a few minutes more, hon. Are you getting hungry?" Angela inquired.

"No, but I want to play ball. My Sunday School teacher told me we would."

"If Mrs. Fletcher told you that, then I'm sure you will," Angela responded with a certainty about another human being that she rarely displayed. She glanced at Adam, and wondered if she'd ever be able to trust him that way. What a refreshing possibility.

What she couldn't know was that Adam was wondering the same thing. Only he suspected that earning her trust now would require more truth from him than he was ready to reveal. And what did the Lord require from him so early in this relationship? Honesty, he knew, but in how large a dose at a time?

Soon they arrived and parked in the gravel alongside her parents' car. Judging from the vehicles already there, it was a good turnout, as usual. Adam helped Angela unload the items she had brought, as well as the case of soda he had placed in her van. Before long, the kids were engaged in a softball game and it was time for Adam to meet Angela's parents.

"Mom. Dad. This is Adam Dalton," Angela introduced her date. She had advised them earlier of this impending meeting.

Smiles from Grace and Ed Granston did little to ease the tension of the moment. No man would easily receive the approval of this older couple where their daughter was concerned. Angela was no kid, but she would always be their child. Exactly who was this Adam Dalton who threatened their daughter's freedom and peace of mind in the wake of her unhappy marriage? They both prayed Angela would find a loving man and marry again someday—but the *right* man.

"Hello, Adam." Grace spoke first, but Ed did extend a hand in an almost friendly fashion. "It's nice to meet you."

"It's good to meet both of you, Mr. and Mrs. Granston."

"The name's Ed and this is Grace," Angela's father answered in a somewhat gruff voice. "Let's find a seat around here somewhere."

They unfolded the lawn chairs they had brought with them and, after greeting and speaking with some of their friends from church, settled into a comfortable place to watch the kids play ball. And to talk. Adam hadn't needed to meet anyone's parents like this since—he couldn't even remember the last time. Unless, maybe with Patty.... But that had been years ago.

So the long day began with introductions and discussion about everything from Ed's real estate business to Adam's log home that his brother had helped him build last year.

"I didn't know you were good with carpentry work," Angela stated. "How did you get started with that?"

"When I was a teacher, I spent part of my summers helping my brother with his home-remodeling business. I've even been on a few missionary trips to South America to help build churches and parsonages for the nationals there."

Ed's face lit up on that comment. "I've been on a couple of those trips myself, Adam," he began. And Angela and Grace shared a secret smile and both leaned back in their chairs. Once Ed started reliving his travels, it would be a while before he stopped. Fortunately, Adam could relate to many of the stories and seemed to enjoy the lengthy conversation.

"Mom!" Heather called when, nearly an hour later, she ran over to where Angela sat. "We need another player. The other team has two grown-ups on it, and we're getting pounded out there. Could Adam play?"

"What? You mean you don't want *me?*" Angela asked.

"Get real, Mom. You know you can't pitch." She looked over at Adam, who had already stood up to join her. "Can *you?*"

"Yep, let's go," he replied. "Excuse us, we'll be back after we win this game."

Angela watched them cut across the playing field. She saw Adam touch Heather's shoulder and then point her in the direction of first base.

"I like him, Angela," Grace stated quietly and with a confirming smile. "Very much."

Ed cleared his throat roughly. "I have to agree with your mother. I like him, too, but it will take you a while to really get to know him. Probably a year or two."

Angela looked over at her father instantly. "A year—" She stopped speaking when he laughed affectionately at her surprised expression.

"I wouldn't want you to rush into anything," he added before squeezing her arm lightly, "but maybe a year or two would be asking a lot."

"Anyway, Dad, I'm just trying to decide whether to continue seeing him—not whether or not I want to spend the rest of my life with him."

"But you shouldn't date him unless he is a man you *could* spend the rest of your life with...if you chose to," Grace commented. "Don't let yourself fall in love with someone you're going to have to say goodbye to in the end."

"Find out about his past and what his plans are for the future," Ed added. "I don't want to see you hurt again."

"Dad, I'm not sixteen. I know the risks." As Angela watched Adam in the distance with her children, those risks didn't seem to loom so dangerously. She liked nearly everything about him, regardless of how much she didn't want to. Angela was beginning to wonder how it would feel to be with him, not just the way they were today—awkward, uncertain—but rather, how it would feel to belong to him with familiarity, confidence. How would it be to sit next to him tonight without wondering if she'd ever sit next to him again? Did she trust the Lord enough to allow Him to give her this new possibility? Could she trust Adam?

"Dinner!" The loud announcement brought the players in from the field and most everyone else to their feet. Soon the crowd gathered around the tables that had been set up and covered with paper plates, napkins, plastic forks and spoons, bottles of condiments and bowls of potato chips and other side dishes. There were coolers of soda pop and pitchers of iced tea. The children were hungry, and they came running to meet Angela and get into the line for their sandwiches, hot off the grill.

Adam walked up to stand close by Angela as the pastor announced loudly that it was time for a prayer to thank the Lord for their meal and this day. Adam reached for Angela's hand, linking his fingers through hers. She looked up, surprised—but pleasantly so—by his action. His smile in return was warm and gentle...and brief as he lowered his head and closed his eyes for the prayer. Angela did the same with a heart filled with gratitude. She'd seen other couples holding hands like this during prayer. In earlier years, she had been a little envious. Then she had either stopped noticing or stopped caring. But this time was different. It was her turn, it was Adam's hand—and something felt very right about his touch.

Soon they were eating hamburgers that were overcooked and baked beans that were barely warm. The kids opted for hot dogs, which seemed to have been the wiser choice since they ended up going back for seconds.

When the meal was finished, David, Nathan and Heather all headed in the direction of their friends, and Angela and Adam sat down once again with the Granstons. That's when Ed's questions became a little unnerving for Angela: he asked Adam about previous marriages. Adam had one, he explained without hesitation. It had ended in divorce.

"And children?" Ed inquired.

"No children," Adam answered quietly and more politely than Angela thought her father deserved. She decided that it was time to take action.

"Okay, guys, it's getting late and, Dad, you're getting a little too personal. Help me round up my kids before it gets dark so we can head home." She leaned near Adam and whispered, "Save my place. I'll be right back."

Adam offered, "I'll go—"

"No, please, stay here. Let Dad help me find them. I want to talk to him about his investigative work," she remarked.

His mouth curved into a smile in response to her comment. Then he squeezed her hand before letting her go.

"It's hard for Ed not to nose into his children's business," Grace stated after Angela and Ed were out of hearing range.

"I understand," Adam responded. "I'd be the same way if I had a daughter."

"I believe you would. And I say that as a compliment, you know."

"I know," he replied. "And I want you to know that I really like Angela. It's been a long time since I've had anyone significant in my life, but Angela...."

"...could be significant?" Grace suggested with a mother's smile.

"Yes," Adam concurred and studied the gentle

face of this older woman across from him—a face much like Angela's might look twenty years from now.

"You're a wise man, Adam Dalton, and you have great taste in women." Grace stood up, and Adam did, too. "I'm going to try to catch up with those two and help with the children. Thanks for coming here tonight. I'm sure you could have done something more enjoyable than being at this church gathering of people you don't know, meeting us, eating hamburgers that tasted like lighter fluid."

Adam laughed. "Mine wasn't so bad."

"Well, mine was," Grace remarked, "but fortunately, I wasn't very hungry. They never seem to get someone to grill the meat who actually knows what they're doing." She reached out and touched Adam's cheek. "We hope to see you again soon."

"You will," he answered.

Grace nodded, and left him to join her husband and daughter.

Adam stood at the edge of a group of people gathered around the bonfire, and watched Angela cross the grassy area toward him. She hugged her corduroy jacket closer as the chilly air of the early October evening settled in.

"Where are the kids?" he asked when she neared.

"Mom and Dad offered to take them for a while." She looked toward the dwindling crowd. "And they all wanted to go." Then Angela raised her gaze to study the shadows falling across Adam from the roaring fire close by. His eyes seemed more distant than she'd noticed before, and she looked away.

"The temperature has dropped since the sun set," he remarked. "Do you want to walk up where it's warmer?" He touched only her coat as his hand moved to her arm.

"No," she said a little too quickly, and then paused. She wanted to say it right. "I...I'd like to leave now." Her cautious blue eyes returned to meet his dark gaze.

Adam searched her face in the flickering firelight, then responded with no more than a slight nod. He clasped her hand in his and gave an easy tug.

They walked hand in hand across the gravel parking lot. Angela kicked up some pebbles with the toe of her boot, while Adam slid the key into the lock, and opened her door. She smiled up at him through the twilight. Even in air rendered smokey from the bonfire, she was close enough to enjoy the spicy scent of his cologne, and it filled her with unfamiliar longing. As she moved past him toward the passenger seat, her right arm and shoulder brushed against his chest in an unintentional contact that jolted her. Her hand flew up spontaneously, involuntarily to touch the front of his shirt. Never before could she remember wanting anyone's kiss as much as she wanted Adam's in that solitary moment. And it took all her willpower to pull away from him and climb into the van.

Adam looked away from her toward the subdued light of sunset in the western sky, giving no indication that he had noticed the awkward moment. Then he shut the door and walked slowly around to the driver's side to join her in the vehicle.

Angela looked straight ahead, staring steadily out the window. If she so much as glanced his way, he would read these emotions in her eyes. No feelings this strong could be hidden for long, she knew, but if they could get away from here—all the people, cars coming and going, the kids, her parents.... If they could be alone, some place, any place, private—even if only for a few minutes.... If he kissed her, she'd know how he felt about her. She closed her eyes momentarily at the thought of Adam *not* kissing her, and sighed audibly. That couldn't happen. Surely he felt something similar for her, didn't he? These feelings in her didn't arise out of nowhere. Their beginning was with him, in him, from him.

Adam drove in silence for several minutes. Then when they did speak, they did so sparingly. Had she enjoyed the evening? Would he join her for another cookout? Mostly they rode silently in the hush of evening for the quarter of an hour it took to reach the large white garage directly behind Angela's apartment. But to Angela, it seemed her heart had been racing for far longer than fifteen minutes.

When the ignition was switched off, Adam got out of the van, walking around the rear of the vehicle toward the passenger side to open her door—as she knew he would. Angela's teeth sank into her lower lip at the sound of his footsteps against the concrete and the lowering of the garage door which shut them off from the rest of the world. What if he didn't feel as attracted to her as she did to him? What if she moved first...reaching for him when his heart was not reaching for hers? Then her door came open. She turned to step out but found Adam leaning in, his hands catching her around the waist as she eased off the seat and into his arms. And for the first time since they left the cookout, she looked directly into his face and discovered the very tenderness she had feared she wouldn't find, waiting there in his eyes.

"I've wanted to kiss you all day," Adam admitted in words that fell gently across her lips. His hands cupped her face, drawing her to him, and his mouth met hers, moving against its softness. She returned his kiss with equal longing. Never in her life had she felt so alive, so wanted. Now. Here. Amid paint cans and bicycles in a cold, dark garage.

But much too soon he let her go.

"I was afraid you didn't feel what I was feeling." The admission rushed from her when she had caught her breath enough to speak. "I didn't know, I couldn't tell—"

"You're driving me crazy, and you don't even know it, do you?" He gave a hint of a smile as he studied the beautiful blue eyes that had so easily captivated him.

"What are you talking about? I'm not doing anything."

"You don't need to 'do' anything, Angela. Just be near me," he explained quietly. "That's becoming difficult enough to deal with."

"Hmm," she responded at the significance of his

words and the feel of his hands resting on her shoulders, stopping her from slipping too far away. "I probably should warn you—you have exactly the same effect on me."

"Good," he remarked, and now it was a confident smile that curved the mouth Angela knew was still warm from her kiss. "That's the way I want it to be. Now, let's go inside your apartment before your neighbors begin wondering why we haven't come out of this garage yet." Adam released her, but not without taking hold of the soft hand he'd already grown accustomed to holding. He grazed her knuckles with a kiss. "C'mon," he said, "let's go."

They walked through the small backyard at a leisurely pace, still holding hands. The autumn air smelled wonderfully fragrant with the scent of apples and wood-burning stoves, and the unraked leaves crunching beneath Angela's boots had never sounded quite as remarkable as they did this night.

They entered the back door to the kitchen, and Angela reached for the light over the sink, although she disliked relinquishing the privacy of the moment. A few more minutes in his arms in the dark would have been welcomed.... Instead she flipped the switch on, and Adam reached for her jacket, helping her out of it before placing it with his own on the hooks by the door.

Angela's first order of business when she returned home from anywhere was to slip off her shoes. Tonight, her boots were no exception. They came off easily and she set them in the corner. Then she adjusted her soft socks and moved to a spot in front of the oak cabinets.

"Sit here with me," she said as she sat down on the carpeted kitchen floor and leaned back against the smooth cabinet doors. She raised a hand to him. "For a while?"

"You like to sit on the kitchen floor," he stated quietly, trying to find logic in her thinking. But he joined her there, logical or not. He placed an arm around her, and she leaned her head against his shoulder.

"When I was a child, I'd sit on the floor in our kitchen sometimes just so I could be alone to think. Now that I have children of my own, I sometimes sit out here with one of them to have a serious talk or to find out what they're struggling with. We usually end up praying about whatever the problem is and then having a snack…right here on the floor. Strange, huh?" she added with a gentle laugh and placed her hand on the front of his shirt much more leisurely than she had done in the parking lot after the cookout.

"We all have our idiosyncrasies," he commented. His hand moved easily to cover hers where it rested against his chest.

"Tell me one of yours," she prompted.

"I'll let you discover mine over time," he replied without smiling.

Time. That was what she wanted with Adam. Lots of it. Was it too soon to feel this way? Probably. But she couldn't help it. She just did.

"Your father asked me some important questions

today,'' he stated, a solemn look stealing over his expression. ''Questions it would have been all right for *you* to ask, you know.''

''With a dad like mine, I don't need to ask. He's quite a detective, and his prices are very reasonable.'' She smiled. ''So, you've been married,'' she stated softly. She had not been surprised. She'd felt certain there was a specific woman, a special love lost, or some other heartache she might not be able to ease.

Adam's hand closed a little tighter around hers as he pulled it away from his chest and placed it on the floor, his hand still resting snugly against hers. Angela watched his restless movement and wondered what he was thinking…remembering.

''Who is it I need to know about?'' she asked, waiting for the name she didn't really want to hear.

''Patty,'' he said and squeezed her hand. ''I was in love with her for a long time. We married when we were in college.''

''And…?''

''It didn't last. We'd only been married about a year when she found out she was pregnant.'' He paused, collecting his thoughts. This was only the beginning of what he needed her to know. ''Patty didn't want to have the baby, but…the idea of an abortion just because this child was coming at an inconvenient time in our lives didn't feel right to me. I wasn't a particularly moral person then; I wasn't raised that way. But an abortion didn't seem fair to the baby, and that's what it was to me—a baby.'' He hesitated again, remembering. ''So I talked her out of it.''

"And you stayed together? She had the baby?"

"Yes. We stayed together and adjusted to the idea of being parents. We even went through the childbirth classes. By the time he was born, I actually felt like a father."

"A little boy," Angela commented and thought of the birth of her first son. Nothing she could think of was as wonderful, as frightening, as overwhelming as having the doctor hand that tiny infant to her in the delivery room. And never before had she felt such a wave of love wash over her. She was linked to her children in a way that she never would be free of—nor would she want to be. She looked at Adam's grim expression and suspected it was much the same for him.

"Brandon," he quietly stated. "He was healthy and strong and beautiful." He looked down at Angela's hand as he continued. "The first six months were rough. We had classes, jobs, studying to do...and a baby to care for. Patty and I pretty much divided up the time with Brandon so we could each meet our other obligations." He stopped talking for what seemed an eternity.

She studied Adam's profile as he continued to look down. "Those early months can be difficult," she commented needlessly, rather than enduring the silence.

Adam laughed gently. "There was never enough sleep, Patty and I had no time for each other, and there was always more to do than there was time to do it. I guess if I hadn't loved them so much, the marriage probably wouldn't have lasted as long as it did." He paused again. "And in all those months, it never occurred to me once to ask if the boy was mine."

Angela winced. "Oh, Adam...how awful." She had considered possible endings to his story, but this hadn't been one of them.

He nodded and laughed harshly. "Yes, it was awful. I didn't believe her at first. I hoped she was lying to try to get out of our marriage. But after the blood tests, I knew it was true. Brandon was the son of a co-worker of hers that she'd apparently been involved with off and on for a couple of years. His wife found out about Patty and divorced him. Since he was free, Patty wanted to marry him."

"And you let Brandon go," she said, knowing his answer before hearing it.

He nodded again. "There wasn't much I could do to prevent it. I wanted to make the marriage work, and I tried to convince Patty to stay with me. I wanted to adopt Brandon and be a family...be the family I had *thought* we were all along. But she wasn't interested, and Brandon's biological father wanted him. The law was on their side. Brandon wasn't my son—at least, not in any legal way. The court deals with facts, not feelings."

"I'm so sorry. I can't imagine how you felt." Angela spoke softly. "Do you ever see him?"

"No. I haven't seen him since he was eight months old," he replied with a slight shrug of his shoulders. "It wouldn't do either of us any good." He looked up and met Angela's sorrowful gaze. "It's in the past and that's where it belongs."

"But how can you trust anyone again after what happened to you?"

"It took a long time to recover from that. I did a lot of stupid, reckless things I'm not proud of, but one night I was watching television when a preacher came on and began talking about hope...forgiveness...starting life over again. Something gripped my heart in a way I can't begin to explain. I got down on my knees right there in that apartment, and prayed—something I'd never done before in my life."

Angela raised a hand to touch the corner of the smile that had begun to curve Adam's mouth. Then her fingers moved down to his shoulder. "You trusted God."

"Yes, and I knew He'd forgiven me and that He wouldn't give up on me from that day on." Adam's smile widened and he leaned forward to brush Angela's forehead with a kiss. "And because of that, I'm here with you."

"Trusting me," she whispered.

"You have to learn to do that, Angela, even though it's not easy when you've been hurt."

"It's more me I can't trust than you," she explained. "My judgment of things—"

"Men?" he asked.

She nodded in agreement. "My marriage was not a good one, Adam. Not even in the best of times. Dan finally left me for someone else."

"You're afraid of that happening again? With me?" he asked quietly, carefully.

"I don't know specifically what I'm afraid of. I just know that what I'm feeling for you now—what I've felt since that night at the Open House—frightens me. I didn't want another relationship. I wasn't looking for one."

"Neither was I, but here we are, knee-deep in something that looks suspiciously like a relationship," Adam said quietly. "Funny how things like that sneak up on you, isn't it?"

Angela smiled, alleviating some of that worried look that had creased her brow. "Funny? Maybe. Frightening? Definitely."

"It doesn't have to be, not with us." Adam's warm hand touched the softness of her cheek. "We're not kids, Angie. We won't make promises we can't keep. We'll go slow, get to know each other, be open and honest...." His smokey gray eyes lowered to her mouth as he spoke.

"Honest, huh?" Angela remarked almost without thinking. Honesty would require her telling him how much she wanted another kiss like the one they'd shared in the garage. But it seemed that her clear gaze had already told him. "Adam," she began, then edged a fraction of an inch closer before he closed the gap between them. His mouth brushed hers, softly at first and then more confidently, as both of her hands moved to rest against his shoulders. But before their kiss became more, it was brought to an abrupt end by the sound of a car pulling into the driveway.

"Your parents," Adam said as he reluctantly released her. They stood up slowly.

Angela looked out the window and nodded. "With my kids." She smiled, watching them pile out of their grandparents' car and run toward the back door. Those children were her life, and had been for what seemed like forever. Where would her need for Adam fit into that scenario? Nathan might never adjust to the idea of a male authority figure in his world again—at least, not one beyond that of his grandfather or perhaps one of his teachers at school.

"Adam?" She spoke his name quietly and turned to see him move to open the back door for her approaching family. Her concern over so many conflicting feelings could be plainly read by him.

"It will be okay, Angie. Just give Nathan some time. He's not ready to deal with this yet."

Not yet, Angela knew. And maybe never. If that was the case, she'd walk away from what she could have with Adam. Giving the children a happy childhood—for what was *left* of their childhood—was her plan. She could not undo all of the emotional damage Dan had inflicted, but she would do what she could, no matter what the personal cost to herself. She had settled that issue in her mind long ago.

Adam sensed a determined spirit in Angela. It was one of the qualities that had attracted him to her, and he realized the significance of it. It was one of the things that could keep them apart. Of course, there were others. At least one.

He was polite but brief with his greeting to Angela's parents and children when they entered, but he left as soon as he felt it was acceptable to do so, with no more than a smile in Angela's direction as he departed. The steering wheel he touched was cold when he climbed into the cab of his pickup. He started the engine and moved the defroster to warm. Then he thought of Brandon—someone he used to think of often but rarely did anymore. He remembered giving him that warm bottle of formula during those middle-of-the-night feedings, his warm little body snuggled close and his sweet baby smell. He remembered how Brandon would look up at him, his eyes full of trust and contentment, seemingly studying Adam's face for as long as he could keep those little eyes open—which was never until the bottle was empty. He remembered how it felt to love a son.

"Lord, You know I'd have done just about anything for that boy," he said quietly in the silence of the truck. Including staying in a marriage with a wife who didn't love him. "Angela is exactly the same. If we're going to work this out, if we're right for each other...You'll have to help us with Nathan. And help me find the right time—soon—to tell her... everything." Then he headed home to the house that would feel empty tonight, more so than it had yesterday. Or any of the days that had gone before.

Chapter Five

It was early the next afternoon when Angela picked up the ringing telephone. "Hello."

"Hi," Adam answered, "how are you?"

His voice was low and quiet, the way it usually was, and the familiar sound brought an instant smile to her lips. "Fine. And you?" she asked. For being 2:00 on a Sunday afternoon, her day was going incredibly well. The kids—all three of them—had their homework done, lunch was over and the kitchen cleaned up. Angela had another administrative report to go over before tomorrow morning, but it could wait.

"I'm okay," he responded. "I have to go over to the center for a couple of hours, but first I wanted to thank you for yesterday."

"For sitting on the floor in the kitchen with you?" she asked with a smile as she sat down at the dining room table.

His laugh was gentle. "The kitchen was good," he remarked, "and the cookout...and the garage."

Hmm, yes, the garage. That was good, but she couldn't bring herself to say it so plainly. Aloud. Over this phone. "I had a wonderful day, Adam. Honestly."

"Me, too. The kids okay?" he asked.

"Yes, they're all right. They had fun."

"What about Nathan?" Adam asked. He hadn't missed any of the glimpses of negativity Nathan had shown on Saturday, and he was concerned about every one of them.

"He seems fine," Angela replied, but she knew how Nathan *seemed* and how Nathan really *was* inside could be two very different things. "He is very good at masking his emotions." Where did he learn that anyway? Angela glanced at a mirror hanging on the nearest wall to see the answer to her own question staring back at her.

"He's a boy who misses his father," Adam commented. "I doubt if he'd be open to the idea of spending time with me—hiking, golfing— I don't even know what he likes to do."

"Nathan and Dan didn't really spend much time together. He loved his dad, but they weren't especially close. I don't know whether the absence of a doing-things-together kind of a relationship with Dan makes Nathan more likely or less likely to do something with you."

"I'm not going to try until he knows me better. Let's plan something for next weekend that we can all do. How do you feel about fishing?'' Adam asked. ''Do you think Heather would be okay with that idea?''

''Heather will scream at first sight of a worm, but other than that—since it's something *you* suggested—she'll be delighted to go. She seems quite smitten with you, if you'll pardon the use of an antiquated word.''

''I like antiquated words. I think some of them come from our generation. And the only person I actually know who is 'smitten' is me.''

''Good. Mission accomplished, I guess I should say,'' she remarked with a smile. ''So, fishing next weekend. Right?'' Next weekend, she thought as her smile faded. It seemed so far away.

''Yep, weather permitting,'' he responded. ''Now, how about us? I can't wait a whole week to see you. Would lunch tomorrow be possible?''

Angela's lips curved back into a comfortable smile. ''Yes. Would 11:45 work for you?''

''That's fine. My schedule is flexible. Should I pick you up in front of the school?''

''No, there's a parking lot in the back of the building for staff members. Pull in there, and I'll find you.''

''See you then.''

'''Bye,'' she replied, and hung up the phone. Tomorrow would be the first time this year that she'd leave the school building to have lunch. Maybe she could slip away for an hour without feeling guilty. Skipping her usual peanut butter sandwich, eaten at her desk wouldn't make her less of a principal, would it? Being a workaholic wasn't in her job description unless it was to be read somewhere between the lines.

Of course, she thought, lots of things in life are exactly that—hidden somewhere between the lines. That definitely had been true with Dan. Sylvia had been the last such surprise. Angela certainly had not expected that. She hoped that whatever kind of relationship she and Adam shared in the coming days, it would be one of few surprises.

The next morning at school was filled with returning phone calls, two meetings with parents and a discussion with several teachers regarding a conflict in class activities as scheduled on the school calendar. The issue of an impending transportation problem was tabled when a bell rang signaling the end of fourth period. 11:45 a.m.

"Gretchen, we'll continue this discussion when I come back from lunch," she advised her secretary as she reached for her purse and car keys.

"You're going out?" the young woman asked. "Is this a special occasion?"

Angela nodded her head as she started toward the door. "Yes, I'm having lunch with...a friend."

Her secretary smiled and took a seat at the front desk. "Male or female?" she asked, her green eyes wide with curiosity.

"His name is Adam," Angela responded. She looked back over her shoulder at the attractive blond secretary she'd worked with since taking this position, and decided she'd made a good decision in meeting Adam outside the building.

"I thought I detected a little more perfume on you than usual this morning."

Angela stopped in her tracks. "Too much?"

"No," Gretchen responded with a light laugh. "It's just right. Do I get to see this guy?"

"Not yet." Angela turned the knob to let herself out of the office.

"Then when?" Gretchen persisted, watching her boss exit in an obvious hurry.

Angela glanced back over her shoulder. "After you gain about thirty pounds, age five years and cut that gorgeous blond hair." She was pulling the door shut behind her just as Gretchen was saying something about Angela's lack of self-confidence, a popular topic of her secretary's. "I know, I know," Angela responded, and closed the door quietly behind her, leaving the lecture unfinished.

Adam's truck was parked next to her van toward the side of the lot, and he was standing outside reading over some papers he held in his hands. He looked up at the sound of her approaching. "Hi," he said, smiling broadly.

Angela smiled back. "Hello," she replied, feeling suddenly bold. If she followed her instincts, she'd lean forward to kiss him on the cheek, but sensibility prevailed. She resisted. Stuffy, old-fashioned sensibility. That and the fact that Gretchen was probably staring at them through the mini-blinds in the office window.

"Where shall we go?" Angela asked, and brushed some imaginary lint from her dark blue dress. The color accented the shade of her eyes. She wanted to feel attractive today, and from the admiring look in Adam's gaze, she guessed she'd succeeded.

"Do you like pasta?" he asked, when he could recall the question he was supposed to be answering. "There's a great restaurant a few blocks from here that I've been to several times."

"Then let's go there," she responded, as he opened the door to the truck cab for her.

"I think I'll try the lasagna." Angela gave her order to the waitress. "And an iced tea, please."

"Salad dressing?" the young woman serving them asked.

"Italian, please," Angela answered, then listened to Adam order his spaghetti. In only a moment or two, the waitress was back with freshly baked bread and butter for them to enjoy while waiting for their orders. Angela cut into the warm loaf and shared it with Adam.

"Mmm, I love homemade bread," she commented after the first bite. "My mother is a wonderful baker. Cinnamon rolls, whole wheat bread, biscuits...all kinds of delicious things."

"Does she have one of those bread-making machines?" Adam asked.

Angela laughed. "I'd love to see her expression if she heard you ask that. She'd be highly insulted, I'm sure. Mom is usually very contemporary in her thinking, but some things just don't sit well with her. Using a machine to make homemade bread is one of them. She's a 'baked-from-scratch' person until her dying day.''

''I suppose we're all a little set in our ways at times,'' he responded, just as the waitress delivered their salads and drinks. ''So...have you inherited your mother's talents in the kitchen?''

''Basically, I hate baking,'' Angela confessed. ''And cooking doesn't exactly thrill me either, though I try my best for the kids.''

Adam laughed. ''I appreciate your honesty. Is this a warning about your cooking?''

''Not at all. My cooking tastes okay,'' she answered with a grin. ''I haven't lost a dinner guest yet, anyway. But don't expect a pie unless it's a special occasion.''

Their meals were delivered to the table promptly and they were actually able to eat and leave within less than an hour. But it would take far more than a lunch hour to continue their conversation. Angela felt as though she could talk to this man forever and still have thoughts she wanted to share, things she wanted to know about him.

''Thank you for lunch,'' she said as they pulled into the staff parking lot in back of her school. ''I enjoyed it very much.'' She looked over at him, and he smiled as he covered her hand on the seat between them with his own.

''Could we do this again later in the week?'' Adam asked.

"Tomorrow would be good," she replied. He obviously was interested, perhaps as much as she was, and she wondered how long that would last. She'd seen loves that she thought would exist forever—most of them in her own family—but she'd never considered what it might be like to be a part of a relationship like that, to live with that confidence in her heart. "I should go," she said. "Tomorrow?"

"Same time, same place," he answered. Then he squeezed her hand. "I'm assuming that there's to be no kissing the principal in this school parking lot?"

"You've assumed correctly," she responded. "I could lose a lot of leverage with these kids if they began to view me as kissable." She smiled and reached for the door.

"I'll get it," he said and got out to walk around to her side and open the door. "See you tomorrow."

She nodded as he squeezed her hand and then let it slip from him. He returned to his truck and headed back toward the center for the remainder of his workday. He'd be there until closing tonight, missing Angela the entire time. He missed her already, even though the seat across from him was still warm from where she'd been seated moments earlier. What was happening with them? He hadn't asked for this. There'd been no prayer from him that the Lord might lead him into a relationship like this. He'd been fine alone. Content. Busy.

Lord, what's happening to me? he silently prayed. *Why have You sent Angela Sanders into my life, out of the blue?*

Blue. He'd never seen eyes a prettier shade than hers. He could spend a lifetime with this woman if only she could accept a part of his life that he'd learned to accept. He'd meant to warn her in the beginning, but the falling-in-love part had caught him off guard. That, and the fact that there never seemed to be a right time to tell the woman you love that you're fighting a battle that can only be won a day at a time.

Their lunch dates that week were brief but fun. Angela couldn't remember eating better food, laughing more, or enjoying better discussions with anyone more than she did with Adam. They had their differences, but they also thought alike on many subjects, including most spiritual matters. "Spiritual matters." Angela could hardly believe this was really happening. Over the years, she'd learned not to share her religious views with Dan rather than endure the flippant remarks that were sure to follow. He didn't care that she and the kids had been as deeply involved in church as his own parents were during his growing up years. That had been Angela's business, not his. But he certainly didn't want to hear anything about a God he didn't believe in. For Angela to now find herself seated with a man who loved the Lord—a man who might love her and her children some day—was almost too wonderful to believe. Why God would be so good to her after all the times she'd failed Him still mystified her.

The weekend was nearly upon them, and Adam was planning to take Angela and the kids fishing Saturday morning at Spring Hollow Lake, a favorite place of his about an hour from their home, and Angela was looking forward to the day. Adam would need to be back at the center Saturday evening, but that would give Angela and the kids time to themselves, which she knew they needed. Especially Nathan. For him, Saturday would probably come too quickly.

The drive didn't seem long that morning. Heather and David were sleeping, and Nathan was in his own little world listening to his radio through headphones and flipping through a book about karate.

"I've brought plenty of food, I think," Angela remarked as she rummaged through her large purse to find her sunglasses.

"Pie?" Adam asked as he tilted his head to one side with a mischievous look.

"Brownies. They're much quicker."

"This isn't a special enough occasion, huh?" he asked.

"Sorry. For pies, we're talking Thanksgiving, Christmas...something major." He'd have to stick around until the holidays, and Angela's hopes were certainly headed in that direction. But at that moment, Nathan reentered their world and interrupted with some questions about a stock-car race track they were driving past. Angela couldn't help but wonder if his timing had been as deliberate as her comment had been. Maybe he was more like her than she thought.

Finally, they reached their destination. The coolers

and the laundry basket Angela used to hold picnic supplies were carried to a large rectangular table standing in a grove of trees. A few forlorn-looking autumn leaves needed to be brushed from the tabletop before Angela could put down the plastic cloth she had brought. Adam took the children down to the water's edge and, one by one, got them set up with bait on the hooks and poles in the water.

Surprisingly, David had a bite right away and, although the large bluegill got away, it created a lot of excitement for them. David was certain he'd be reeling something in before the day was over. Adam sincerely hoped he would. It wouldn't be much fun for them if they didn't catch anything. After spending about an hour with them, he decided to go back up to the picnic spot where he could see Angela sitting. They could safely see the children from that vantage point.

"You need help with anything?" he asked when he approached her.

"No, thank you," she replied. A fire was already going in the grill and there were hot dogs and hamburgers on a plate nearby, waiting to be cooked.

"I thought you'd ask me to get the grill started," he commented, noticing the expression of satisfaction shining in her eyes at a job well-done. "I guess you're doing fine without me."

"I don't think I'll ever be fine without you again, Adam." The words sprang from the bottom of a heart that he had filled with love and contentment. She was certain, now, that she was in love with him, and almost as unsure of where it would take them. Or if the Lord was leading the way.

Adam touched her face, brushing a few wisps of dark hair from her cheek. "I feel it, too," he responded in a low, almost husky whisper. "Very much." The tenderness in his expression was enough to quiet her concerns for the moment.

Heather came running up the hill into their area, right toward Adam and into his legs, grabbing him and bringing a laugh of surprise from both adults at the interruption.

"What are you doing?" Angela asked.

"Mommy! Adam! Help! David's chasing me with a caterpillar. A big yucky black one!" she exclaimed.

"Well, tell him I said to stop. And to put that caterpillar back where he found it," Angela stated firmly.

"The poor thing probably wants to go back home to its family," Heather added and took off back down the incline to pass along her mother's instructions.

Adam moved away from Angela as he turned to watch Heather race back down to the lake. "She's growing up very much like you did. A little girl with two brothers," he commented.

"But she's probably equally close to both boys. For me, for some reason, I always felt closer to Rob."

"Why?" Adam asked as he reached for a soda pop and opened the can. Just as he did so, the carbonated beverage overflowed from its container and ran over the sides and down his hands. He and Angela both laughed in startled surprise at the incident, and the kids came running to see what the commotion was about.

"Maybe carrying them over that bridge and the bumpy ground shook them up too much," David observed. He had been the one who'd carried the small cooler, so he was the most likely of all present to know how shaken up the container had been. "Sorry."

Adam and Angela were both assuring him that it didn't matter. There was no harm done. Adam wiped his hands on the wet cloth Angela handed to him.

"With three kids you never go anywhere unprepared," she remarked as she pulled out her plastic bag of supplies. Wipes, bandages, paper towels, shoelaces, safety pins, tablet and pencil, juice boxes and graham crackers.

"You pack snacks, too, for emergencies?" Adam asked as he looked over the items she was sorting through.

"If I get stuck in traffic or have car trouble, I'd rather let them have a drink—even a warm one—and a few stale crackers than listen to the woes of three hungry passengers."

"That makes sense," he answered, and watched the children—who'd lost interest in the spilled beverage—amble back toward their fishing spot. "Some of it sprayed on your clothes," Angela observed. She automatically reached to wipe at the stain across the front of his long-sleeve shirt and down his left arm. "And on...your arm...." Her heart thudded loudly, ringing in her ears, and she berated herself silently for being so profoundly affected by her actions. But affected she was, and her touch on his clothing remained. She wanted to kiss him; she wanted to even more than she had the other night after the cookout.

Adam knew her feelings instinctively. He'd have known even without the hesitation in her touch or the catch of breath in that beautiful, slender throat of hers. He reached for her wrist, stopping her movement and drawing her attention up to his stormy gaze. The urge to kiss her almost overwhelmed him as the floral scent of her perfume filled his senses. And those eyes... Adam thought he might drown in that summery blue. He couldn't recall falling so fast for anyone. Ever.

Just over Angela's shoulder and in Adam's direct line of vision were the children. His attention shifted from her lovely face to the three kids with fishing poles in their hands. When his eyes met hers again, he released her wrist slowly. "Nathan," was all he said, and all he needed to say to snap Angela back to reality.

She nodded in mute understanding as he turned from her. He opened the cooler and rummaged through it until he found the iced tea. Reaching for a cup, he smiled over at her. "Maybe this will be safer than the soda."

She cleared her throat. "Should be," she replied. She knew she was blushing. What Angela would have liked to do was put one of those cold, unopened cans of cola against the side of her face. As if it weren't already obvious enough to him the impact that his nearness could have on her. Angela glanced at the kids when she heard Heather scream.

"It's only a worm! Shut up or you'll scare all the fish!" They heard Nathan shouting at his little sister.

"Nathan, go easy on her," Angela called out to her son, then began setting out the food she had brought for their lunches. "Sandwich buns, chips, drinks...where are the brownies? Did the kids get into them in the van?"

"I don't know," Adam responded as he helped her search through their belongings. "Here, in this box." He produced the plastic container with dessert inside.

"Thanks. The children will be asking for them."

"Angela, you were telling me about your brothers before the soda ran over. Why are you closer to Rob?"

She wiped her hands on her jeans. "I don't know. He was older, protective. And our minds kind of worked alike I guess. Eric was rowdy. Not terribly rebellious...still something of a loner. Now Rob—he can be as aggressive at times as he needs to be, but underneath it all, he's really very sensitive and tenderhearted." She rolled up the sleeves of her blue-and-green plaid flannel shirt. "It's warming up. It's hard to believe it's October."

Adam looked past the picnic table and across the wide grassy expanse leading to the lake, whose waters remained calm and still. "It's a perfect day for this. I just hope the kids actually catch some fish."

"They had a couple of bites when you were down there with them earlier, didn't they?" she asked and continued pulling paper plates, cups and other necessary items from her basket.

"Yes. I think I'll see how it's going." He touched Angela's forearm as he moved past her.

Angela finished getting food on the table, and about ten minutes later, Adam and all three children returned to their picnic area to eat. Fishing tips became the mealtime topic, and the boys' opinions differed. As usual.

"You've only been fishin' a few times, Nathan, so don't act like you know it all," David stated after listening to his brother's talk a little longer than he cared to. "How many times has Grandpa took—"

"Taken," Angela corrected.

"...'taken' you fishing?" David asked.

"More times than he's taken you. That's for sure."

Adam listened to more than what the boys were saying. He considered the things they weren't saying. No mention of their dad taking them fishing, showing them how to use the bait or take a fish off the hook once it's reeled in. How could Dan Sanders have had these two young boys in his life and seemingly have done so little with them? What a loss for all of them. A sharp twinge of remembering pierced Adam's heart. Adam and his brother had grown up in much the same fashion. But at least their father's illness had been something of an excuse. He couldn't imagine what rationale Dan Sanders might have used to avoid a close relationship with his sons.

And Angela? She seemed to Adam nearly too good to be true. What could possibly have gone so wrong within her marriage? She didn't seem open to discussing it. Adam knew every relationship had its problems, it's own uniqueness, but why did it seem everyone was so closemouthed about Angela and Dan's? He wondered if Tiffany knew any more about Dan than he did. Probably not. If she did, she'd already have told him. And asking—that would seem gossipy.

"What time do we need to leave for you to make it to work?" Angela asked, studying Adam's thoughtful expression. "I don't want you to be late."

"Let's stay for about two hours if the kids are enjoying themselves. That would leave me time to shower and change before I have to be there."

Those two hours went by quickly, especially once everyone started catching fish. When departure time arrived, the boys both were asking to come back again. Soon. Heather wanted to know if next time they could fish with something less disgusting than wet, wriggly night crawlers. She thought something dry and plastic would be much more acceptable. The trip back to Angela's was uneventful, and Adam helped unload the van once they had parked up near the garage. It didn't take very long, considering all the stuff they had packed. And all three children helped after only a little prodding from Angela.

"Well, I've gotta go. I'm due at the center in ninety minutes," Adam said, walking out of her house. He wanted to drape an arm around her shoulders and pull her closer as they headed toward his truck, but he wouldn't right now. Not in broad daylight with the children all around. They stepped onto the driveway, and Adam did reach down to take her hand—as if a touch would in any way placate his longing for this woman.

"Thanks for spending time with the kids. The boys are desperate for that kind of attention."

"My pleasure. Nathan didn't seem as out of sorts today as he was last weekend." Adam didn't want it to be just his imagination. Things had seemed better, hadn't they?

Angela smiled. "He'll come around. He needs time to learn he can trust you."

Trust. There was a subject Adam wasn't ready to delve into. Nathan needed to trust him, Angela needed to trust him...everyone needed to trust him a lot. Now. Before he had to ask them to trust him later.

"I hope he warms up to the idea of having me around. *Soon,*" Adam emphasized the word. "It's important to me. And I know it's important to his mother."

"I'm hoping that day comes soon, too." She squeezed his arm and watched him climb, slowly, into his truck and shut the door. He didn't want to leave; she could see it in his every movement. And it only made her love him more.

"Hey, Adam!" Heather called as she rushed up to the truck. "When I get my award for swimming this year, will you be there? All of us want you to come."

Angela and Adam both laughed a little. "Honey,

Adam is the director of the center. Of course, he'll be there."

"But, Mom, I don't mean will he 'be there.' I mean will he *'be there?'* You know, to see *me?*"

"Yes, I will be," he answered. "And are you going to dive so you can move up to the next class?"

Heather shrugged. "I might, if you help me."

"When you're ready, I'll be there," Adam promised.

"And come to the ceremony for Mom, so she won't be lonely," Heather added. Then she threw a quick "See you later" over her shoulder as she took off to rejoin her brothers.

"Think you'll get lonely sitting in those bleachers all by yourself?" he asked.

"Actually, I should be used to it. I've gone to plenty of their programs alone over the years. And this time the boys will be with me."

Adam was quiet for a moment, thinking of the parts of life he and Angela had both missed, but each for different reasons. "I'll go with you to the children's programs as much as my schedule allows, if you like."

She tilted her head to the side slightly, studying the look of concern she saw in his eyes. "I'd like that very much."

He hadn't even left the driveway, and yet he was wondering when he would see her again. "Tomorrow would be too soon, I think," he said as he started the engine.

She nodded. "They're used to having me to themselves on Sunday. I don't think they're ready to give that up yet. What about lunch on Monday?''

''Can't. I have to be at the center. And Monday night I have a meeting to attend downtown. How about Tuesday?''

''Nope,'' she responded, crossing her arms and leaning in through the window he'd rolled down so she could kiss him lightly near his ear. ''I have a luncheon to attend. Let me check my schedule for the week. Then I'll call you.''

He put the vehicle in gear to pull away. ''And that wasn't the kind of kiss I had in mind.'' Not even close.

''I know. Me neither,'' she replied and moved away from the door. A gust of autumn wind blew swirling leaves of various colors across the driveway and around her feet as he left.

''Do you want to rake leaves, guys?'' she asked. They all had too much energy to go inside now, so they may as well have some fun and get some work accomplished at the same time.

''Yes!'' the three replied enthusiastically. They headed toward the garage to gather up a couple of rakes and a push broom, and Angela joined them in creating a huge pile of leaves that Heather and David immediately dove into.

''I wish we had a dog like we used to,'' Nathan said to his mother when she pulled a few stray leaves from his windblown brown hair. Last fall, when they had raked the yard at their own house, Max had been there jumping into the piles of leaves with them.

She looked into Nathan's eyes—blue like her own—feeling a pang of guilt. "We can't, honey. Not in this apartment." She looked up at the four-unit building where they had resided since the divorce proceedings began. When their former house had sold and the bills had been paid, there hadn't been enough money left for a down payment on a smaller house. So she had chosen this apartment. "The lease on this rental specifically states that no pets are allowed." But that was only part of the reason they no longer had the little black-and-brown stray that Nathan had named Max. The animal had run away from them one morning after Dan had disciplined the dog too harshly for growling. Angela refrained from commenting much about the pet's disappearance since the day it happened because she didn't want to lie to Nathan, and neither did she want to tell him exactly what had happened.

Max had felt threatened by Dan for good reason when Dan had come home in the early hours of a Sunday morning after spending Saturday night with his friends. Drinking. The dog had only been protecting Angela and the kids from the intruder Dan appeared to be. Dan had been angry and speaking loudly to her, and it must have alarmed Max more than usual. Dan had been verbally abusive to her at times, but he'd not acted in any way that was physically threatening to Angela or the kids. She wouldn't have stayed with him if he had. No, she'd stayed because he didn't want her to leave, or so he said. And she stayed because, for a while at least, she hoped he'd change. The Lord could have changed him if Dan had only been open to the idea of the existence of a higher power, of the God who could have helped him.

"Do you think the Lord understands how much I miss Max?" Nathan asked quietly.

Angela slipped her arm around the boy's shoulders and kissed the crown of his head. "I'm sure He does, hon. And some day, when we own a house of our own again, you can have another pet."

"You mean, if Max doesn't come back?"

Angela bit her lower lip and nodded her head. There seemed to be no point in reiterating to him that Max would never come back. Or that if the dog did return, he would naturally go to their old house across town instead of coming here. Nathan had resisted that idea at every mention of it. So she relented. "Yes, if Max doesn't come home, you could have a different pet." That seemed to be enough to soothe Nathan for now; he once again began raking the leaves his siblings had scattered across the lawn.

Later, when they had finished their work in the yard, they went inside for the evening. Everyone was tired from the fishing trip and the two boys needed the first showers. They'd gotten much dirtier than necessary when helping Adam clean the fish at the lake and put them on ice for the trip home, and their clothing reeked with fragrant evidence of their participation.

When David come out of the shower, he rubbed his hair vigorously with a towel. "Adam said he'd freeze those fish so we could go over there to eat them some night. Have you ever been to his place, Mom?"

"No, I haven't," she responded, reaching for the hair dryer on the shelf and switching it on. "But I guess we'll *all* be going over there for a fish dinner pretty soon."

"I hope so," David stated. "I like Adam."

Angela smiled as she dried his black hair, running her fingers through it a few times. "I like him, too."

"I don't see what's so great about him," Nathan grumbled as he headed toward the bathroom.

"You liked him fine when you were taking karate last summer," David retorted. "What's wrong with him now?" David and Angela both looked at Nathan, waiting for his answer.

"Everything," Nathan stated before disappearing into the bathroom and slamming the door.

"Nothing!" yelled David.

"Okay, okay, you guys. Knock it off." Angela placed the hair dryer on the stand in the hallway. "Nath, the hair dryer is out here when you need it," she called through the closed door. "And no more door slamming, please!"

"What's the matter with Nathan, Mom?" Heather asked when she went to Angela for a hug. Arguments and disagreements of any kind usually sent her running to the safety of her mother's arms. "Why is he so mad?"

Angela smoothed some of Heather's dark hair from her forehead and kissed her there. "Sometimes it's hard to adjust to something new in your life."

"Like having Adam around?"

"Adam is not a 'thing,' goofy," David commented.

"I should have said 'someone' instead of 'something.'" Angela corrected.

"Adam is a good someone to have around," Heather said with a smile. "I like it when he's here."

"That's what I like about him. He's *here.*" David emphasized the word, and Angela watched his young eyes cloud with sadness before he turned from her and went into his bedroom, adding, "Dad hardly ever was."

"Nathan's mad, David's sad and I'm glad," Heather said suddenly. "We sound like a poem."

"Yes, you do. Now go get your clean underwear and pajamas from your dresser. Nathan will be out of the shower in a few minutes, and you're next." Angela swatted her daughter lightly on the bottom as the girl followed the instructions without argument.

Angela knocked gently and stepped inside the bedroom her boys shared. "David? You okay?" Her son was looking through a red book bag with a decal of a shiny race car on the front zipper pouch. "I'm okay." He looked up. "Why?"

"You seemed kind of upset when you came in here. I thought maybe you wanted to talk. About Adam. Or about your father."

"Nope. Nothing to talk about. It's just that...I like Adam. I'd like it if he hung out with us more. You know, did stuff with us, like today. That's all." Then David turned his dark brown eyes to the interior of his book bag. "Have you seen that white caterpillar I found at school yesterday?"

Angela shook her head. "I didn't know you had

one,'' she answered, ''but if you've left him in that book bag all day, he's probably no longer alive. He wasn't one of those fuzzy ones, was he?''

''Yes. And that was his name. Fuzzy.''

''David, I asked you not to play with those things. You know the pediatrician said they can give you a bad rash. If you find him, I want him out of here. Tonight. Understood?''

''Okay,'' he replied reluctantly. ''If you say so.''

''I say so.'' Angela turned, only to come face to face with Nathan wrapped up in a towel.

''Excuuuuse me,'' he said as he made his way through the doorway and into his room. ''Mom, I've gotta get my clothes on.''

''Okay, I'm out of here.'' Angela left, closing the door behind her. She wondered if the boys would discuss Adam when they were alone in there. Probably. And which one would be the influential one? Probably David. He wanted to be the attorney in the family, and his arguments at times could carry a lot of weight, even with his siblings.

''Great,'' Angela muttered under her breath as she went to check on Heather. ''I'm relying on a ten-year-old to sway a jury of one: Nathan. Lord, if You're listening, I need some help on this. If You're trying to show me Your will, I'm not getting it. Couldn't I just have a lightning bolt, or, maybe, some handwriting in the sky? *Yes, Adam Dalton is for you,* or *Stay away from that man.* Either one I could handle. Then, at least, I'd know.'' At least, she'd know.

Chapter Six

Tiffany leaned in through the office door. She found Adam going over schedules for the winter session, quietly whistling some tune.

"So, you really like this Angela Sanders, don't you?" she asked with a smile.

He looked up from his work. "Yes, I do. I'd like for Allen and your mother to meet her soon."

"I don't recall your introducing anyone to the family before. That serious, huh?"

"Could be," he replied, then noticed his niece still standing there as if there was something she wanted. "Do you need me for something?"

"I wanted to tell you there were a couple of college guys that stopped by earlier. They're interested in possibly teaching some classes next summer—swimming primarily. I asked them to come back this afternoon. You'll be here, won't you?"

Adam nodded. "Until 9:00 tonight. What are you

doing in here, anyway? You're supposed to be off today."

"I had a few things to catch up on, and I wanted to see Cameron. We need to decide on wedding invitations."

"Ah, yes," Adam said with a hint of teasing in his voice. "The wedding. Are things working out as you had hoped?" He leaned back in his chair with his hands casually folded together behind his head.

"Goin' fine. The only hang-up is my dress. I can't seem to find exactly what I'm looking for. Everything seems so...so...."

"So...what?" Adam asked. "Expensive? Conservative? White?"

Tiffany laughed. "All of the above. But the funny thing is I kind of like that reserved look. You know what I mean? Like the way your Angela dresses. She always looks so...grown-up."

"She is grown-up, but she's not *my* Angela."

"She could be," Tiffany remarked, "if the way her face lights up when she's around you is any indication."

Adam barely heard the reply. He was busy thinking how pretty Angela looked every time he saw her, regardless of what she wore. Even that old sweat suit she'd been wearing the first night they met somehow had managed to look appealing on her. Soft, warm, comforting. Her nose was red and her eyes were watery, and if he hadn't been so angry at her for leaving Heather without a ride home, he would have wanted to help her. Some way.

"Adam?"

He heard Tiffany call his name and realized he'd been ignoring her, lost in his thoughts. He returned his gaze to his niece's serious expression. "Sorry."

"Have you told her?"

Adam's heart went cold. He was head-over-heels in love with a woman who didn't know one of the most important basic facts about him. "Not yet," he replied, sitting up straighter in his chair. When had his past become a secret? He'd always meant to tell her; he just hadn't gotten around to it yet. He was waiting for the right time. That was all.

"You'd better fill her in before you bring her over to Mom and Allen's. You never know how something like that's going to go."

Adam cleared his throat. "True," he answered. "I'll talk to her."

She raised her dark eyebrows in cynical question.

"Soon," he answered her unspoken question. "Soon."

Tiffany turned and left him alone—with schedules, telephone messages and guilt. Lots of it. Angela needed to know, but he couldn't deliver news like this on a one-hour lunch break. They'd need an evening alone, with no time restrictions, so they could talk—*really* talk—and determine where they would go from here. He would invite her to dinner at his house. Maybe Ed and Grace could watch the kids. He'd take care of it…soon. But right now, there was something else he'd had in mind since last night.

* * *

Angela picked up the phone on her desk as soon as Gretchen mentioned the caller's name. "Adam? Hi. What a pleasant surprise."

"I know you said you have a luncheon to attend today, but could you get away for about ten minutes if I come over now?"

"Now?" She glanced at her wristwatch. "Sure, I guess so. Why?"

"I'll explain when I get there."

"I'll watch for you to pull into the staff parking lot," she responded.

"Thanks. See ya." He picked up his keys. "I'll be back in less than a half hour," Adam told Tiffany. "If that new sports equipment comes in while I'm gone, sign for me, but make sure you look over the purchase order and see that we actually got what we ordered for a change." Then he was out the door and on his way to school.

"Adam? What's going on?" Angela asked when she met him in the lot.

"Get in." He motioned for her to join him and leaned over to push open the door for her.

"I can't leave for more than a few minutes—"

"That's all it will take. I want to show you something at the library. It's across the street." He put the truck in reverse to turn it around and traveled the short distance. Within minutes, he parked in the narrow lot, and was out of the truck, opening the door for Angela.

She laughed lightly. "Adam? The library?"

"Yes. This is a very educational kind of place. You're a principal, so you'll fit right in here."

"What are you talking about?" she asked, but she held tightly to the hand he'd offered and wasn't about to let go until she figured out what this was leading up to.

They neared the front door and it opened automatically. "This great idea occurred to me last night while I was in here for a meeting."

"A meeting? What kind of meeting?"

"That's not important," he said and squeezed her hand. "It's the conference room that I want you to see."

"Hello, Mr. Dalton," said an older woman who occupied the checkout desk. "Mrs. Sanders, good to see you again. May I help you in some way?"

"Hello, Mrs. Perkins. Is anyone in the conference room?" Adam replied.

She shook her head. "It's empty."

"I just wanted Mrs. Sanders to see it," he explained briefly. As the librarian nodded her assent, Adam was already ushering Angela down a shelf-lined hallway. Then, past a water fountain and elevator entrance until they reached the last door on the right. Adam pushed it open and stepped inside, tugging on Angela's hand and pulling her easily into the place he wanted her to be—in his arms. The door quietly shut behind them.

Suddenly she realized this was Adam's great idea. A place for them to be alone. Even if only for a moment or two. A gentle smile curved her lips as she glanced around the dimly lit room; only slivers of light made their way through the drawn blinds. "This?" she asked, just to be sure.

"This," he responded, his hands slipping up her arms, drawing her to him. And then he was kissing her, gently at first, almost as though she was fragile, delicate...as if she could break in his arms. But Angela's response assured him that she was none of those things. She was real enough—a woman who missed him when he was away and who thought this brief excursion to the library was the most romantic thing he could have done. Then he was tenderly touching her hair, her face, her shoulders. "Angie, I don't know how long you expect me to go between these kisses, but today—right now—is the limit for me."

She sighed softly in agreement and opened her eyes to meet his gaze. "Privacy...it's like a prized possession in my life."

"I know," he said quietly, his warm fingers caressing her cheek in a wistful gesture. "But I can't kiss you at noon in a crowded restaurant. I won't kiss you in front of the kids—not yet anyway. And I'm certainly not going to come anywhere near you when we're at your school." His hands edged slowly down her arms. "So I guess we need to reserve this room at the library," he said, a mischievous smile replacing the earlier melancholy expression she'd glimpsed in him.

Angela's laugh was soft, gentle. "Or you could invite me to dinner tomorrow night. I'll ask Mom to watch Heather, and maybe Dad could go to soccer practice with the boys. The kids wouldn't even miss me for an hour or two."

Adam leaned close, brushing her temple with a light kiss. "I'll see if Tiffany will trade a couple of hours with me then. Now," he added, "as much as I hate to, I need to get you back to work, don't I?"

Angela placed a hand on his chest to feel the steady pounding of his heart. Then, reluctantly, she agreed. "I'm already a few minutes late."

"Sorry," he commented and reached for the door, pulling it open slightly and allowing some light to spill in.

Angela smiled. "There's lipstick on you," she said, with some satisfaction. She rubbed the corner of his mouth with a thumb to wipe away the evidence and, just for a moment, let her mind wander back to the fishing trip. And the soda pop. "You know, at the lake last weekend...." She paused, wondering how much of her feelings she should admit to him. It was all so new to her, so wonderful, so unexpected.

"...you wanted to kiss me," he completed her statement with calm assurance, "and probably not half as much as I wanted to kiss you."

She looked into his tender eyes. "But—"

"I understand about the kids. It wouldn't be good for Nathan to see me becoming too familiar with his mother. Not yet."

She nodded, looking down at the gray carpeting at her feet. Was she moving in the right direction for her children or was she thinking only of herself? And Adam?

"Nathan misses his father," Adam commented, then hesitated. "Do you?"

Angela raised her eyes instantly in wide surprise at the question. "No," she said with almost too much emphasis. "He hurt all of us and made life difficult. In a lot of different ways." None of which she wanted to discuss now. Her life and the children's were back in order again, mostly thanks to the absence of Dan. She'd even given up attending the weekly support group she'd belonged to for years—for spouses and family members of alcoholics. For the first time in her adult life, she didn't qualify, and it felt wonderful.

"Actually, it's you I miss," she said rather boldly, and moved her hand down to his strong grasp. "I can't take these days apart very well either, you know."

"Maybe we won't have to very much longer," he offered, knowing he was saying more than he should. But she had a way of rousing thoughts of forever in him...something no one had done since his college days. Not since Patty and Brandon.

"Let's go—" she squeezed his hand "—we have a real world to get back to, you know."

"Unfortunately, you're right," he answered, pushing the door open the rest of the way and stepping out into the hallway with Angela's hand wrapped warmly in his. He glanced down at his watch. "Sorry that I've caused you to be late for your luncheon," he said, showing her the time.

"I'm not," Angela remarked as they moved through the hallway of the library and out toward the sunshine in the parking lot. They returned to the school in a matter of minutes, and Adam opened the door of his truck to let Angela out.

"I'll call you about dinner tomorrow." He smiled. "Enjoy the rest of your day."

"I'll try," she responded before leaving him.

She would try, but it was becoming increasingly clear to her that her days with Adam felt better than the ones without him. And her nights? She sighed. She wasn't even going to think about those.

Angela wasn't thinking about much of anything, later in the day, except Heather's queasy stomach and climbing temperature. The stomach flu that so many people had suffered from recently had come on quickly. The boys were still visiting at a friend's house when Angela's body began aching, too. She stuck the thermometer in her own mouth as she ran tepid water over a washcloth and placed it on Heather's scorching forehead. When it had been in for only a minute or so, she pulled it out to look at the numbers: 102 degrees. Heather's wasn't registering that high. "Mommy, I think I'm going to throw up again," Heather called out on her dash to the bathroom. Angela rushed to help her. It was nearly nine o'clock and someone had to pick up the boys. So she called the first someone she could think of: Adam.

Chapter Seven

"Mom, the kids...." Angela said with a hoarse voice. Her throat, raw and scratchy, barely let her speak her mind.

"They're fine, honey. The boys are with Adam, and Heather is sleeping. Her temperature is down to 99.5 now."

"Thank the Lord. She was so sick."

"She's not the only one. And we *should* thank the Lord—and Adam, too. He's the one who called me," Grace Granston explained to her daughter.

"I didn't want him to—I didn't want you to worry."

"Nonsense, worrying is what mothers do best. Three kids of your own, Angela...don't you know that by now?"

"I suppose, but—"

"But, nothing. When you need help, you call me. That's an order," Grace said. "Did you know that your Adam stayed with the children while I took you to the E.R.?''

''Mom, he's not 'my' Adam.''

''He could be,'' Grace answered with confidence. ''I like him, Angela. Very much. How are you feeling now that your fever has broken?''

''Better. Different,'' she said. ''I felt so disoriented last night.''

''It's no wonder, as high as your temperature soared. Heather wasn't half as sick as you were. Her fever started going down before I even got here. This twenty-four-hour virus hits hard but leaves fast, and that's the only good thing that could be said about it,'' Grace said. ''I'll get you something to drink.''

''No juice, please. My throat feels horrible.''

Grace nodded her head, disappeared into the kitchen and returned with a jumbo-size glass of crushed ice and tea. ''This ought to taste pretty good.''

''Thank you,'' Angela responded and took a large swallow of the cold liquid. ''I don't know what I'd do without you.''

''I guess you'd need to rely on Adam more,'' Grace answered without hesitation as she leaned over and straightened Angela's blanket. ''Have you realized you're in love with him yet?''

''Definitely, completely,'' Angela said between sips of iced tea. ''Hopelessly.''

''Have you told him?''

''No,'' she said.

''You need to discuss that with him,'' Grace answered with a smile and a pat on her daughter's leg. "I don't think you ought to let this man get away."

"Since when do you interfere in your kid's love life?"

"Interfere? With you? When did I have time to do that? You had little more than started dating Dan when you came home, crying and pregnant. You were married and a parent before you even knew what a grown-up relationship could be."

Angela sighed. "Mom—"

"Well, it's true. You had no idea how special or loving or just plain fun the whole thing can be. And considering the way Dan treated you, I doubt that you do even to this day." Grace sat down in a chair close to her daughter.

"Mom, why are we having this conversation? Dan's gone—"

"We should have had talks like this all along," Grace interrupted. "Even when you were very young. I don't know why I thought that even without talking about things they would somehow turn out all right." She paused. "Do you remember those books we gave you when you were about twelve?"

Angela thought for a second. "You mean those little books about the facts of life?"

"Exactly. I don't know why I took the easy way out. I should have talked to you about that instead of letting you read about it."

"Mom, why are we discussing this?"

"Because I want you to do a better job with Heather than I did with you."

"Heather and I talk about everything."

"Everything?"

"Well, no, not *everything*. Maybe not in depth. Not yet, at least. She's only six years old."

"Six isn't what it used to be. Be more open with her than I was with you," Grace suggested.

"Especially with the don't-get-pregnant-and-embarrass-your-family part. Right?" The sting of the past sharpened her words.

"No, I was never concerned about gossip or any of that. The only person you hurt was yourself. That's what broke my heart." Grace gave a bittersweet smile. "That's all I really cared about."

Angela's eyes misted with tears.

"I want you to do a better job with your kids than I did with mine. And I want to see you in a happy marriage. It's your turn."

"I'll try. Honestly, I will. But I'm thirty-two years old. I gave three children and twelve years of my life to Dan. I don't think I have much left to offer Adam."

"Nonsense," Grace replied. "Give him your heart. You've kept it to yourself far too long."

"Mom, how did you know..."

"Know what? That you never loved Dan? That things weren't right between you? Honey, I knew from the start. When you finally did really care about him, it was more of a watching-over-him, wanting-to-help-him, wanting-him-to-change kind of affection." Grace leaned forward to touch Angela's cheek.

"I wanted to love him. He was my husband, the

father of my kids. And they loved him very much. They still do."

"I know, but when he left you, I was glad. I knew you'd be too stubborn to ever leave him."

"I guess I was glad when he left, too, but I didn't want him to die. I hoped he'd be happy with Sylvia, if she was what he wanted," Angela responded. "The Lord knows he was never happy with me."

"But Dan is gone, regardless of how we feel about it. And you're free to love and free to marry. So do that for me. Make your mother happy by being happy yourself for a change." Grace smiled and stood up. "And my guess is Adam Dalton is your man."

"I don't know, Mom. He's almost perfect. Sometimes it scares me. How could things be so good?"

"Wait until you've married him. You won't believe how good things can be," Grace commented with a sly smile. "That's how God intended."

Angela reached for her glass of tea without responding. Her mother was right, she knew. She really had no idea how a relationship like that could be.

Grace frowned at the silence. "You and Adam—you're not..."

Angela nearly choked on her iced tea. "Mom! I'm thirty-two years old!"

"I didn't ask your age. I asked if—"

"You *can't* ask me personal things like that," Angela stated flatly.

"I can ask you anything I want. Whether you answer or not is up to you." Grace stood, waiting for a reply.

"No, of course we're not," Angela said with a sigh. "Mom, give me a break, will you? I'm an intelligent woman, a mother, a Christian. Do you think I have no regard for living a Christian life-style? For myself? In front of the children? I'm not the same stupid college kid who got into trouble."

"I know you're not. Forgive me for asking, but I worry about you. You're not a kid, but you're still my child. You'll see how this feels when Heather is grown up." Grace sat back down, pushing some brown hair behind an ear. "Adam is exactly the kind of man I had envisioned for you to marry."

"Well, I may not be what his mother envisioned for him, or even what he envisioned for himself—a woman with three kids to raise?" Angela ran a hand through her disheveled dark hair. "I must look awful."

"Not awful enough to scare him away," Grace said with a smile. "He was here all last evening helping with you and Heather, both sick with the stomach flu. If he didn't love you, that would have been the right time to make a quick exit, don't you think?"

"I guess you're right. God is so good to me, I don't know why He'd give me another chance. Especially with a man like Adam. I don't even know if I could be a good wife to him. I'm not certain I know how."

"You'll figure it out, one step at a time," Grace assured her. "I'm going to check on Heather again. I want you to sleep."

"But what about David and Nathan?"

"They went home with him after you and I came

back from the emergency room. He's taking them to school, as long as they both feel okay. They didn't show any signs of catching this bug last night. Now, you get some sleep. Adam will be over later to see you, and I'll leave you two alone for a while,'' Grace stated.

''Thanks, Mom,'' Angela said, and reached out to clasp her mother's hand. ''I love you.''

''I love you, too, dear.'' Grace squeezed then released Angela's hand, and she headed for the hallway. Before disappearing around the corner, she added, ''Remember when I asked if you'd told Adam you were in love with him yet?''

Angela nodded. ''Yes.''

''I think you should tell him soon. He deserves to know.''

''I'd rather wait until he tells me.''

Grace stood there thoughtfully for a moment. ''I think, in a way, he did last night. The way he was with the kids, with you—''

''Mostly, he was with the kids, Mom. I was too sick—''

''That's the point. You were much sicker than Heather. I was the one who said I'd go to the hospital with you and that he should stay with the kids. He deferred to my judgment—since I am your mother—but, looking back on it, I'm sure he wanted to take you to the E.R. himself. I guess I was just the worried, meddling mother who stepped in and changed the plans. Since you have allergies to some medications, I wanted to be with you to make that clear to the doctors and nurses. But I should have trusted Adam to do so. I apologize for that."

"Mom, it was fine that you were with me. Don't apologize for caring too much."

"I'm not, but I'm beginning to think Adam may be as reluctant to trust you as you are to trust him. If that's the case, this could be a very slow-moving romance you've embarked on here."

Angela laughed lightly. "That's what you and Dad wanted for me, wasn't it? Something I wouldn't rush into?"

"Yes, but...." Grace's smile had a mischievous slant. "You don't have to crawl along at a snail's pace either, you know, dear."

"Right, I'll keep that in mind," Angela answered before leaning back onto her pillow. Keeping Adam in mind wasn't difficult to do, but it did make sleep absolutely out of the question.

"Hi. Feeling better?" Adam asked when he arrived later that morning. He bent down on one knee beside the sofa and placed a hand on Angela's forehead to check for fever.

"Much better," she responded, reaching up to squeeze his fingers.

"You're much cooler. Your fever must be gone—the worst of it, anyway." He picked up the thermometer from the coffee table. "Have you or Heather used this thing this morning?"

"Yes," she answered with a smile. "Mom's been looking after us, and we're both doing fine."

Just then, Grace came out of the kitchen. "Morning, Adam. I think our patients are both on the mend."

"That's what I wanted to hear," he replied. "You're probably exhausted. Go home and get some rest. I'll keep an eye on things around here. I won't need to leave until about three to pick up Nathan and David from school."

"Yes, Mom. Go home, rest, quit worrying," Angela encouraged, as Adam and Grace moved toward the front hallway.

"I am really tired. I guess my age is finally catching up with me. Angela, stay in bed and take care of yourself. Adam, Heather is asleep in her room, and Gretchen called from school asking that Angela call the office sometime before noon. But don't let her do that much. The moment she can stand without fainting, she'll be up trying to do the laundry or cook or something."

Adam took Grace's jacket from the coat hook, and held it for her while she slipped her arms into the sleeves. "I'll take care of her, Grace. Don't worry."

She turned then and looked him directly in the eyes. "I know you will. You've already proven that to me...several times over." She touched Adam's arm with an approving pat. "She's crazy about you, Adam. Don't let her tell you otherwise."

"You know the inside story on this?" he asked, a skeptical frown creasing his brow.

"I know my daughter," Grace replied and then paused. "She's afraid of being hurt again." She turned to the door that Adam pulled open for her. "She has a hard time trusting anyone."

Adam's expression brightened with a smile of acknowledgment. "That's not something you needed to tell me."

"What are you talking about?" Angela called from her makeshift bed on the living room sofa.

"Goodbye, dear," Grace responded to her daughter with a mischievous smile aimed at Adam. "I'll let you answer that question," she whispered before slipping out the front door.

"Thanks a lot," Adam said quietly.

"Adam?" The soft voice came from inside.

He closed the door. "I'm right here." He returned to the couch where Angela was resting.

"What were you and Mom talking about?" she asked suspiciously.

"You," he answered. "And us," he added with a kiss to her crown. "I think your mother likes me." He sat down on the edge of the sturdy oak coffee table.

"Likes you?" She shook her head and laughed. "She wants to *keep* you...permanently."

"And what do *you* want?" he asked, point-blank. All hints of a smile faded.

Angela wondered how she could say the things she felt. There were no adequate words. Not in all the world. "I want to keep you, too," she said softly and watched Adam's smile warm to match his eyes. "But I'm afraid my mother will scare you away with her plans for our future."

Adam caught her hand in his own and kissed her lightly across the knuckles. "Nothing has scared me away yet."

"Not even how terrible I look?" She spoke her thought aloud. No makeup, unkempt hair, the same old nightshirt she'd worn over her jeans to the emergency room last night.

Adam's smile broadened, and he shook his head in assurance. "You look like you're feeling better, and that's all I care about. Now, do you feel like having something to eat? Tea and toast maybe?"

"That would be nice," she said as she pulled the blanket away from her. "But let me shower and change clothes first so I feel more like a human being."

"Can you stand up all right?" He extended a hand and stood up with her, supporting her by the elbow. "You're still a little wobbly."

"I'm okay," she insisted and took a few steps toward the hallway, pulling away from him. "I'll feel better if I can clean up."

Adam crossed his arms in front of him. Grace had been right. As soon as Angela could possibly stand up, she was off and running to get things back to normal. "Angela," he began as she glanced back at him, "don't overdo it. Your mother suspected you would as soon as you were capable of standing."

"My mother, the worrier."

He nodded in agreement. "A trait you've undoubtedly inherited from her," he said with a smile. "Go clean up, and I'll check on Heather."

"I'll do it, Adam. I'm headed back toward her room anyway."

"Nope," he said as he caught up with her in the hallway. He put his arm around her shoulders and kissed her temple lightly. "You shower and change while I look in on her. After all, that's what I'm here for—to be helpful."

Helpful, Angela mused as she bit her lower lip. He was already too helpful, too kind, too easy to kiss. And that shadow of a beard.... She wondered how that roughness would feel against her cheek. Grabbing some clothes from her bedroom, she went into the bathroom for a long-awaited shower. She *must* be in love to think this way. "But then, I don't have much to compare it to, do I?" she reminded herself out loud.

Soon hot water was splashing over her head, through her long, limp hair and down her weary body. How long she stood there, thinking of possibilities, with her eyes closed and her forehead against the cool blue-tile wall, she wasn't sure. "Oh, Adam, what are we getting ourselves into? Three kids to raise and you'll probably want one of your own. Maybe more. Two careers, two homes, two people who won't trust—"

Just then the door to the bathroom opened.

"Mom?" Heather said in a sleepy voice. "Can I take the next shower?"

"Yes, hon. I'll be out in a minute."

Soon both she and Heather were clean, dressed in jeans and sweatshirts, and taking turns with the hair dryer. Then they joined Adam in the kitchen for breakfast.

"There you are." Adam smiled and pulled Heather's loosely fastened ponytail. "Feelin' okay?"

Heather nodded. "I'm hungry."

"That's always a good sign," Angela commented, pouring hot water over a tea bag, as Adam went to the stove and picked up a skillet.

"How about some scrambled eggs to go with your toast?"

"How about a dozen of them?" Heather responded and climbed up onto a tall stool at the counter.

"She's well," Angela pronounced, sipping from her cup. "Are there that many eggs in the refrigerator?"

"Yep." Adam put bread in the toaster. "I brought a few groceries with me this morning."

Angela smiled. She had to find a flaw in this man sooner or later, but she certainly wasn't seeing one here in the kitchen amid delivered groceries and a home-cooked breakfast.

When the food was served, Heather dug in despite Angela's warning not to overdo it. Eating heartily had never been an issue with her; she'd been a good eater as far back as Angela could remember.

Adam filled plates for Angela and himself before they sat down. "And you cook. Does my mother know that about you?" she asked.

"Would it help my case if she did?"

Angela looked across the counter into the deep gray eyes of the man she seemed to want more with every passing moment. "You don't need any help. Mom already adores you. If we ever go our separate ways, she'll probably request visitation rights with you."

He looked up from his plate, meeting her gaze with a silent but warm response. Her pulse quickened as she stared into eyes darkened with emotion. Should she tell him that she loved him? And if she did, what would be his reply? Or would he be ready to give one?

"Do you cook lots of different stuff?" Heather cut into their unspoken exchange between bites of her toast and eggs. "Pizza, chili, chocolate cake, everything?"

Angela returned her focus to the breakfast on her plate, as Adam answered her daughter's untimely question.

"I don't know about chocolate cake or everything, but pizza and chili—those things I can handle," he said. "What's your favorite food?"

"Mom's hamburgers with coleslaw on them and French fries." Heather reached for her glass of milk. "They're even better than burgers at the restaurant."

"That's quite a compliment coming from you," Angela spoke up, now that she could think clearly again. Almost. "Maybe we could have that for dinner tonight."

Heather looked up at Adam. "And maybe you could stay? For the meal, I mean."

A glint of humor flickered in his eyes, and Angela knew he was amused by Heather's awkwardly stated invitation. "Thank you, but I need to be at the center this evening. I'll come by after we close up to pick up the boys."

Angela's eyebrows lifted in question. "I'm feeling well enough to look after them."

"But I promised them they could stay over again. After Grace brought you home from the hospital late last night, I took the boys home with me. They liked using the sleeping bags on the floor in the room with the wood-burner. They thought it was like going camping."

"You sure you want to do that again?" she asked.

"Yes, I like having them around," he answered. He had enjoyed their company more than he had expected, and he had hoped he'd made some headway with Nathan. It was a relationship that needed to be dealt with a little at a time. "I'm going to clean up the kitchen, and then I have some reading I'm going to do while you and Heather rest."

Rest? In the middle of a weekday morning? There's something Angela hadn't done recently, and the idea sounded appealing. "I probably should check in with the office first."

"Yes, do. Gretchen wants to talk to you before noon today."

Suddenly, Angela felt tired. The toll on her from the virus and the fever was registering, and she stopped eating after only a few bites of toast.

"I'm going back to the bedroom to sleep for a while—if nobody objects. I'm exhausted." She started to take her plate and cup to the sink when Adam stopped her, taking the dishes from her hands.

"Go lie down. I'll take care of this," he said. "I'll be here until your mother comes back."

"Mom, can I lie down with you?" Heather asked.

"Sure, c'mon, honey," Angela replied, and they headed toward Angela's room. "Thank you—" she looked back at Adam "—for being here."

Adam nodded, and watched them go. He wanted to be here, now more than ever, but he knew he hadn't yet earned that right—even if he had won her heart.

When Angela and Heather awoke a few hours later, Adam was gone and Grace had returned. He did come by much later that evening to pick up Nathan and David. Then he was gone again, leaving Angela with a new twinge of emptiness. She missed the boys. She'd seen so little of them the past few days. And she missed Adam.

The ringing telephone startled Angela the next morning as she was just about to take a bite of an English muffin. She placed her plate on the counter.

"Hello."

"Hi, it's me," Adam answered, "and I've got a problem."

"Something with the boys?"

"Kind of. The center was broken into last night. I'll fill you in on the details later, but I can't get out of here to take Nathan and David to school right now. Would you let them miss a day to stay with me?"

Angela hesitated. "Adam, I don't know. I don't usually allow them to be absent unless they're really sick. I could pick them up on my way in this morning."

"I know, but—" He paused. "Nathan is really interested in everything that's going on. The police are here and there's a lot of cleanup to be done. If I could keep both of the kids here to help me, I think it would mean a lot. To Nathan, especially."

"You have made progress with him in the last couple of days. I was surprised he wanted to spend a second night at your house."

"So was I," Adam admitted. "I think this could be important today. Will you let them stay?"

Knowing she probably shouldn't agree to the request, she found herself giving in. The boys didn't have any tests that day, and they hadn't missed any school since it had started late in August. One day out of classes couldn't matter all that much. On the other hand, one good day with Adam might make all the difference in the world.

Chapter Eight

"Are you guys all right?" Angela rushed to open the door of the truck, when Adam pulled into the driveway behind her apartment.

"Yes, Mom, we're fine," Nathan answered for all of them, seemingly a little embarrassed by the attention. "Don't worry so much."

Angela put an arm around each of her boys, and then looked up at Adam, her eyes wide with question. "So, everything is okay at the center?"

Adam nodded his head. "Pretty much. The equipment will be replaced by insurance, and I still need to go through some records to determine exactly how much cash was taken. But, basically, things are okay."

"It was awesome, Mom," David said excitedly. "The police were there asking questions and some newspaper people came in to take pictures. We liked it, didn't we, Nathan?"

Nathan shrugged and finally grinned. "It was kind of cool, actually. The storage room was a mess, and there was a window busted out...glass everywhere." He hesitated, then said, "Thanks for letting us see it, Adam. I thought you'd send us home right away."

"There wasn't anything dangerous going on as long as you two stayed out of the glass and I knew I could trust you with that." Adam folded his arms and watched Nathan struggle with whatever it was that he wanted to say next.

"Anyway, thanks," the boy offered. Then he headed for the garage with his brother in close pursuit.

"Nathan's getting so tall," Angela remarked as she watched them go. Her children were growing up, too quickly to please her. She moved to Adam's side. "Thank the Lord everything turned out okay at the center. Nobody was hurt, not much was taken."

Adam tilted his head, studying the concern he saw in her wide blue eyes. "Everything's okay. I'll go back later and go over the records to see if I can figure out what was left in the cash drawer. It couldn't have been much."

"But thank God it was an overnight break-in, not a robbery in broad daylight. Adam, people can get killed over a little bit of money in a cash drawer." Angela felt the sudden sting of tears surfacing, and she turned, moving into his arms and burying her face in his shoulder. "I couldn't bear it if..." Her muffled words trailed off.

Then Adam did something he hadn't done before.

He held her close—out in the open. And no calamity occurred. None. Even though Nathan looked over at them from the garage—where he and David were retrieving their bikes—and Heather giggled when she noticed them as she came running from the apartment to join her brothers. After that, the three kids paid little attention to the adults, and went about their play as if they were alone.

"It's okay, Angie. There's nothing to cry about," he said gently as he rubbed his chin against her soft hair. "Nobody was in any danger, honestly."

She nodded and sniffed, digging into the pocket of her corduroy pants to find a tissue to wipe her nose. Adam was right, she knew. She pulled away from him, chiding herself for being such a worrier. She needed something else to think about. She sniffed again. "How did Nathan act with you today?" she asked.

"Better, I think." Adam thought about the morning, the things that had happened. "Letting him stay while the police were there was good. He seemed to like being trusted that way." Usually Nathan kept his distance from Adam, but today, Adam recalled, he had stood physically closer to him—close enough that at one point during Adam's discussion with the police officers, Adam had rested a hand on the boy's shoulder. Nathan hadn't moved away as Adam had fully expected him to do.

"Really? That's good news. I guess I have something else to be thankful for," Angela remarked, hugging her arms to her stomach to fight off a chill.

"Let's go in," Adam suggested and placed his arm loosely around her shoulders. "It's getting colder out here. You were sick yesterday, and you don't even have a jacket on." He turned to look toward the kids. "Neither does your daughter. Heather, come in here. You need a coat," he called to her. Angela just smiled and accompanied him to the back door. The warmth of the kitchen flowed over them when they stepped inside.

Within moments, Heather came charging into the room. "It's too cold, Mom. I don't want to play outside," she said with a shiver. "I'm freezing."

"C'mere," Adam said, and she eased into his arms for a hug. "You don't feel feverish," he said while touching her face. "Go let your mom see what she thinks."

Angela placed a hand against Heather's cheek and then forehead. "I think you're okay, honey. Why don't you go to your bedroom and put on a sweat suit? That will be warmer than those jeans and that shirt." She tugged on Heather's dark ponytail as the girl turned to follow orders.

"And how do *you* feel?" Adam asked Angela. "You were very sick not long ago. Remember?"

Angela picked up the tea kettle from the stove and began filling it with water from the faucet. "I remember." She placed the kettle on the burner. "I feel fine now. A little tired maybe, but that's all. Want some tea?"

"No, thanks. I need to get going." He stood up and walked to where she stood by the stove.

"Thank you for taking care of us. I don't know what Heather and I would have done without you, other than completely worn out my mother. And I'm sure the boys enjoyed getting to spend two nights at your house." She slipped her arms comfortably around his waist when he took her into his arms.

"I think these past two days were good for them. Nathan is finding it easier to be with me—he's letting down his defenses a little—and David had fun spending the nights in a sleeping bag on the floor. He said he's never been camping."

Angela nodded. "True, and I'm sure he'd love it."

"We'll plan a trip," Adam promised, and kissed her forehead. "Nathan really misses his dog, too. Have you considered doing something about that? Another pet of some kind maybe?"

"I can't here at this apartment. I told him we'd take care of that later, after we find a house," she explained. "He really loved Max."

"I could tell by the way he talked about him. Well, I guess we can think about that later. Call me if you need anything. If I'm not at home, try me at the center." He leaned forward, kissing the soft hair at her temple. "And let's plan to have dinner at my place tomorrow."

"Just the two of us?" she suggested with a smile.

"That would be nice," he answered, and reached into his pocket. "I should be there by six o'clock. If I'm not, here's an extra door key to let yourself in." He turned to go.

"Adam." She hesitated when he looked back at her in question. "Thank you."

He smiled. "You're welcome. See you soon." And with that, he was gone.

It wasn't until later that day, when dinner was nearly ready and Adam was nowhere around, that Angela began to understand the impact the past couple of days had made on Nathan.

"Mom, do you remember how it was with Dad?" Nathan had started the conversation as Angela checked on the pork chops in the oven. "It seemed like anything that went wrong caused a big problem. You know what I mean? If Max barked too loud or one of us broke something...or even when our van quit running...he would always get really upset." Nathan pulled plates out of the cupboard and set the table as he confided in his mother.

"Sure, I remember," she said quietly and wondered what direction this conversation was taking. Nathan probably remembered lots of things about the years gone by that she wished time would erase.

"Adam's not like that," he stated softly. He looked up at his mother as he put silverware beside each plate. "Even at the center today. He didn't make a big deal out of the robbery, never complained about any of it, never told us to get out of his way. He could have. We probably were in his way a lot of times."

Angela didn't respond right away. She was considering carefully what her son had said, and wondering how to answer him in the best possible way. "Adam is calm, patient. He has a very different personality from your father's. And a different perspective on life."

"You mean, because he's a Christian?"

"Yes." Angela picked up several drinking glasses and handed them to her son to distribute around the table. "Things were inconsistent around here sometimes—with Dad, I mean. It wouldn't be that way with Adam." She reached out, touching Nathan's soft hair. He tilted his head, smiling up at her.

"Mom?" he asked. "You're not going to cry now or any emotional stuff like that are you?"

"No," she responded, but not before kissing the side of his face and moving away from the boy she missed holding in her arms. Where had the years gone? "Adam can't replace your father—not in your life or in your heart. But you could have a good relationship with him, if you chose to. He cares about you, a lot." She bit her lip, waiting for his reply and knowing she was probably hoping for too much.

But much to her surprise, Nathan nodded. "I know. I like him, too," he answered, bringing a broader smile to his mother's face.

"Thank you," she offered softly.

"For what?" Nathan asked.

"For being the mature, open-minded young man that I'd hoped you would be." Tears filled Angela's eyes. "I love you."

"I know." Nathan shrugged off his mother's sentiment. "You don't need to start crying about it, Mom. I love you, too."

She hugged him, holding him tightly for a moment and then releasing him. "Go have some fun. I'll finish the table."

"Really? Gee, thanks!" he said and took off out the back door.

"Thank You, thank You, thank You," Angela said aloud to the Lord, who she knew was listening. "How can I ever thank You enough for this?" Adam had been right. Things were better with Nathan now, and it had to be, quite simply, a gift from God.

Just as a life with Adam could be, Angela considered. A lovely, unexpected gift. One that she felt, for the first time, might actually be meant for her.

Chapter Nine

"Hey, Mom! My teacher's sister had her baby. A little girl!" Nathan said from the rear of the van where he and David sat on the ride home from school the next afternoon.

"Already? Isn't it kind of early?"

"Yeah. Two months early," he replied. "Mrs. Mitchell talked to us about babies that are born too soon. She called them 'preemies.'"

"Uh-huh," Angela responded. "Heather, please roll that window up. It's freezing in here." She switched on the heater. "So, Nathan, is the baby okay?"

"Yeah, I guess so, but she only weighs four pounds. That's not much, Mrs. Mitchell says."

"That's very small. But that doesn't mean she won't make it. The baby will stay in the hospital until they're sure it's strong enough and well enough to go home."

"So, I must have been really small like that when I was born," Nathan remarked.

Angela raised her eyes to the rearview mirror to see her son's face. Her heart sank. She'd known someday that they'd have this discussion. It was inevitable. But she hadn't thought it would be today. At age 12.

"Mom, how much did I weigh?"

Angela took a deep breath and let it out slowly. She'd had a springtime wedding and a late summer baby. And Nathan could count to nine. "Hon, let's talk about this later when we have time. We're in a rush to drop David at John's house. And I have a terrible headache." Which was mostly true—she instantly had the beginnings of a migraine.

"But don't you remember how much I weighed?"

"Eight pounds, even," she responded. "We'll finish this discussion later. David, get your stuff together. This is the street John lives on."

After dropping her middle child at his friend's house, she, Heather and Nathan rode home without much conversation. Angela frantically ran over in her aching head the way she wanted to explain things to Nathan. He was the most sensitive and tenderhearted of all her children, and his reaction would largely depend on how well she handled the explanation. At least that's what she assumed.

Their van eased into the driveway and, almost before the ignition was shut off, the doors flew open.

"Heather, change into your jeans before you go outside to play. And wear a jacket."

The two children with book bags and lunch boxes climbed out of the vehicle to cut across the yard, running toward the back door. Angela dawdled behind, picking up her own books and purse slowly and deliberately.

How do you tell a young boy that he wasn't born prematurely? That his parents married a little late? That his conception was the sole reason for their marriage? Angela leaned her pounding head against the door of the vehicle as she stood, stalling, there in the driveway. She'd been sorry for things she'd done, but never sorrier than she was now. But *she* knew it was time to be honest with Nathan.

"Oh, Lord, help me to say the right things...the right *way*. Please don't let Nathan be hurt by this. It wouldn't be fair for him to suffer because of our wrong choices. Please, please give me gentle words to answer my boy's questions."

She stood silently for a moment, thinking of her late husband. Up to this point, she couldn't really say that she had needed his help with anything. He had never seemed to be around anyway for anything that had really mattered—throughout their entire marriage. "But Dan," she spoke his name angrily, quietly, "you *should* be here for this." She slammed the door to the van. "If he's gonna hate me, he should hate you, too." Then she walked towards the back door, the kids—and the truth.

"Mom, we've already had that talk. Why are you bringing it up now?" Nathan tossed his book bag on the floor and sat down on his bed. "What are you tryin' to say?"

Angela cringed, inwardly and outwardly, as she stepped inside Nathan's room and pulled the door shut behind her. Then she began to explain the hard facts. "God has a plan for a man and a woman to marry and have children, creating families. But not everyone lives by the way God wants them to live. Not everyone waits until they are married to…have a child together. But you already know that, don't you?"

"Yeah, there are a couple of teenagers at my school who have babies. They're not married. Do we have to talk about this, Mom? It's kinda embarrassing."

"Believe me, you have no idea how embarrassing this is, Nathan, because…I need you to know that your father and I…."

"Dad and you what? Had a baby when you were teenagers?" he asked with a laugh that Angela did not join in. He looked at her with a quizzical expression on his young face. Then, disbelief. "Mom?"

"We were both twenty when you were born," she stated.

Nathan studied his mother's face as he sat without speaking on his narrow twin bed. "So, why do I need to know that?"

Angela raised the back of her hand to her mouth briefly, considering her choice of words before she replied. "What I'm trying to tell you is that you weren't a premature baby. Your dad and I married in

March, and you were born the last day of August." She watched his thoughtful expression change to one of realization. She hated sharing this truth with him even more than she had imagined she would at least a million times over the past twelve years.

"So you and Dad got married because you were going to have a baby? You decided you wanted to have me even before you were married?"

Angela took a deep breath and let it out slowly. "Well kind of—but not exactly." Would she ever have anything more difficult to explain to her boy in all of her life? She gave a soft smile as she brushed some of his dark hair back from where it lay upon his forehead. Clear blue eyes, the color of her own, stared at her in continued question. "I always knew I wanted to have a son. There's no doubt I would have had you. It's just that...I really hadn't thought it would happen so soon."

"But it did? And that's why you married Dad?"

"That's why we married so young, before we had really gotten to know each other well enough to know if we belonged together—if we could make a marriage work." There. She'd said it. As awful as it was, it was out in the open now for Nathan. The way it needed to be.

Nathan looked down at his book bag and kicked it absentmindedly with his foot. "You didn't want to have me."

"That's not true." Angela sat down beside him on the bed and put her arm around him. But he stood up, shrugging off her gesture of affection and walking to the child's school desk in the corner. Angela's heart ached for him. "I love you, Nathan. I would have had you whether or not your father married me. There was never a question about that. *Never.*"

"But you and Dad weren't happy together. You probably wouldn't have been married if it hadn't been for me." His frown made him look younger, sadder—and brought tears to his mother's eyes.

"You're not to blame for any problems Dad and I had. We created our own problems. You were the one blessing we started out with, and I would marry him all over again to have you...and your brother and sister." Her teeth sank into her lower lip, and her arms ached with wanting to hold her son. "I didn't want to tell you this until you were much older—"

"I wish you'd *never* told me," he muttered as he sat down on his desk chair.

Angela took a deep breath and let it out slowly. "I had to give you an answer about being a preemie. And I don't want to lie to you—not about anything."

"You'd have been just like one of the high school girls I talked about. A girl with a baby. Me."

"I was older than those girls. I was in college. But, yes, I'd have been a single parent if your father hadn't married me." She paused. "Nathan, I've always loved you, but I was young and scared. Your dad and I—neither one of us would have given you up for any reason." She blinked and tears trickled down her cheeks. She wiped them away with her fingers and stood up.

Nathan lowered his gaze to his tennis shoes.

"Could you leave me alone for a while?" he asked in a sharp voice that Angela normally would have responded to with a warning about disrespect. But today she just walked toward the door and opened it slowly. This afternoon she didn't particularly feel she'd earned his respect enough to defend it.

"If you want to talk—"

"I don't," he answered quietly, glancing over at her through eyes brimming with angry tears.

She nodded her head and left him alone, closing the door behind her. Retreating to her own bedroom, she knelt beside her bed to pray. "My help comes from You, Lord. I've read that in the Psalms so many times," she began, "and today I'm asking for that help. I told Nathan the truth. It was the right thing to do. Now, help him accept this news in a way that is not too hurtful to him. Help him to know I love him, Dan loved him...we wouldn't want to *not* have him. Psalm 109:22 says, 'For I am poor and needy, and my heart is wounded within me.' That's true for my son and for me today. Bring some peace out of this situation for us. I've been closer to Nathan than to any of my kids. Don't let his knowledge of my mistakes hurt our relationship in any lasting way. Please, Lord."

She stood up, wiped her eyes and nose on a tissue, and headed toward the back door to check on Heather, whom she found in-line skating on the driveway. It was late afternoon by then, and she had planned to go to Adam's home for dinner with him after dropping off the kids at her parents' home. If she could discuss this with Adam, she knew she'd feel better. Then again, she'd be telling things that she'd rather not tell. As for Nathan, she would give him some time alone to think things through. She poured herself a cup of water and placed it in the microwave. Reaching for the tea bags, she noticed the dirty dishes piled in the sink and the basket of laundry that needed to be folded sitting on the floor in the corner.

Her heart ached to return to Nathan's room, to put her arms around him and cry with him if that's what he needed. But he was not the little boy he used to be. He was nearly a teenager, and, too soon for Angela's liking, he would be a man. She'd concentrate on the housework that demanded her attention now, and give Nathan the privacy he wanted. She wasn't sure if it was the Lord prompting her in that direction, or if it was her own cowardice that kept her from looking him in the eyes right now.

"Mom!" Heather called as she flew in the back door. "I'm hungry. Can I have a snack before dinner with Grandma and Grandpa?"

"Yes," she answered, smiling at her out-of-breath daughter. She pulled a box of graham crackers from the cupboard. "How's the skating going?" She handed a few to the little girl whom she knew from photos was the image of herself at that age—dark, braided hair, sparkling blue eyes, full of life and energy.

"It's going okay. I'm glad for the knee pads, though. Otherwise, I'd be sore!" Heather pulled her sweater off and tossed it onto the back of a chair.

"Where's Nathan? He should go outside. It's nice out."

"He's in his room," Angela replied. "He'll be out when he's ready to do something." And if he wasn't, Angela would go in after him. They were due at her parents' home in about an hour, and she needed to see Adam tonight more than she'd ever needed to see him before—to ask him if she'd said the right things in telling Nathan the truth about his conception. She had, hadn't she?

In thinking of how the Lord would have wanted her to handle it, the truth seemed to be the only option she had. But she didn't feel comfortable with the idea of needing Adam's opinion on this important manner. Decisions had been made throughout her marriage without the help of a man. She'd learned long ago not to rely on Dan's support, and it bothered her now to need someone else's input. Specifically, Adam's.

"Nathan? Honey, are you okay?" Angela rapped her knuckles lightly against the bedroom door. "It's almost time to leave for Grandma and Grand—"

The door pulled open abruptly, cutting off her sentence, and Nathan stepped into the hallway, book bag over his shoulder. "I'm ready," he said without meeting her gaze.

Angela nodded. She placed a hand gently on his shoulder, and he did not shrink from her touch. "If you'd rather stay home tonight—so we could talk—I would gladly do that."

"Nope," he answered as he adjusted the strap on

the bag hanging off one shoulder. "Grandpa would be disappointed. If I'm there, he has an excuse to play video games all evening." And he smiled a little.

Angela nodded again, and smiled in response. She wondered how long it might be before he'd want to have another "real" conversation with her. "You sure?"

"Yes," Nathan said and turned to grab his jacket from the coat rack in the hall. "Let's get goin'."

"All right," Angela replied. "Heather, you ready?"

"Coming, Mom." Her daughter came around the corner with her book bag in one hand and the latest children's video in the other.

"You're not watching that tonight," Nathan informed her before heading out the door. "We're going to hook up the video games after dinner. You know Grandpa and I like to play...." The argument between the kids probably continued after the front door shut and they headed for the van. Angela returned to the coat rack for her own jacket before joining them in the garage. Then they set off in the van for her parents' home, where they were to stay until 9:00. She would pick them up after dinner with Adam.

Adam. She sighed. She could certainly use an encouraging word from him.

Dropping the kids off at Ed and Grace Granston's house took a little longer than she'd planned, so she headed directly to Adam's home when she left. The errands she had meant to take care of—getting cash from an A.T.M. and buying soda pop for the kids—would have to wait until another time.

She had asked Nathan, again, before leaving him with her parents, if he wanted to talk with her alone for a while, or even just go out with her for a burger and a milk shake. But he steadfastly refused. Maybe he was still too angry with her for that right now. She assumed that was it, and she didn't want to force the issue. That might make matters even more awkward between mother and son. Still, she couldn't quite shake the feeling that she should have stayed with Nathan this evening. Or rather, that she shouldn't be going to Adam's house. But she had no idea why, or where the feelings came from.

When she pulled into Adam's wide driveway, she parked behind an unfamiliar vehicle. Adam's truck was nowhere to be seen. She glanced at her watch. He should have been home by now. An even deeper uneasiness settled over her as her eyes came to rest on the license plate of the older-model car in front of her van. Out-of-state tags. Adam hadn't said anything about expecting visitors. In fact, she had not heard him mention even knowing anyone from that part of the country. Darkness had settled in, but lights glowed in the house, and the flickering in the living room indicated the television was on. She hesitated, wondering whether to leave and call Adam from a pay phone to see if everything was all right, or to walk up to the front door and find out for herself.

"This is ridiculous," she murmured, annoyed at

her own growing fear. "All I have to do is open the door and find out what's going on. That's why he gave me the key. So I could get in when I got here." So Angela talked herself out of her instinctive caution, walked up on the front porch, and slid the key into the lock.

Almost immediately, before she even pushed open the heavy wood door, she heard a voice—a decidedly female voice—call out, "Just a minute." Then the door flew open and Angela came face-to-face with a blond, beautiful stranger—a woman about Angela's own age—wearing a large, oversize plaid robe and drying her face with a bath towel. From the expression on the woman's face, Angela realized that the blonde was as startled to see her as she was to see the blonde.

"Oh...hello," the stranger began as Angela stared at her without speaking. "I—can I help you?" she asked, as if she had every right to be standing there inside the front door of Adam's home, looking beautiful and not quite dry.

"Um...yes, maybe. I'm supposed to meet Adam here. I have this key to let myself in.... Who are you?" Angela finally asked. She felt as though she had walked into a movie already in progress and needed someone to fill her in on the first twenty minutes. On second thought, maybe she didn't want to know.

"I'm a friend of Adam's." The blonde smiled.

The plot thickened. Angela frowned and looked away. "I'm supposed to meet him here for dinner," she explained, feeling angry, embarrassed, betrayed. Dinner plans had obviously been changed. Too bad Adam hadn't thought to mention it to her. And apparently, he hadn't mentioned anything about it to this pretty blonde, who seemed quite comfortable here in his house.

"Dinner? Is it that late?" the woman asked in obvious surprise. She glanced at her bare wrist and laughed. "I guess I don't have my watch on."

"No, I can see that you don't," Angela quipped. No watch and not enough clothing in general, she thought.

Angela had already had about all the awkwardness of this situation that she could stomach. "I must be mistaken about the date or the time." Or Adam Dalton, in general. "Sorry to have bothered you." And even sorrier that this other woman was so unbearably attractive with wonderful high cheekbones, wide chocolate-brown eyes and a complexion mostly seen in magazines. And all with no makeup, as far as Angela could detect. Angela, herself, found it difficult to look away from the stranger, and she doubted that Adam would even make the effort.

She turned to go, angry but mystified by this turn of events. How could she have been so wrong about a man? Again?

"But what's your name? I'll tell him you stopped by," the woman called out.

Angela glanced back to see her adjusting the belt of her robe. "Just tell him Angela was here. I'm sure he'll be surprised that I've met you."

Almost as surprised as she was, Angela thought as she looked down at the key she still held in one hand. She knew she could have handed it over to the woman on the spot; instead, she slid it into the pocket of her jacket. This was an item she preferred to return to Adam personally. Probably by throwing it at him the next time she saw him.

Chapter Ten

She pulled open the door.

"It's not the way it looked," Adam stated flatly, skipping any greeting. His expression was dark, almost grim.

"Not the way it looked," Angela repeated. "I am met at your door by a beautiful blonde wearing a bathrobe? How can that be *anything* other than the way it looked?"

Adam glanced past her into the apartment. "May I come in? Are the kids here?"

She opened the door wider to allow him entrance, but only to the hallway. "The kids are at Mom and Dad's for the evening because we had a date. If you will recall, you'd invited me for dinner—"

"Exactly—dinner at my place. Do you think I'd be stupid or careless enough to have some woman there—in my home—then? At the time you're expected to show up?" Adam was inside the apartment now, raking a hand through his tawny gold hair and watching her through troubled eyes.

"No," she answered truthfully. "I don't think you'd have 'some woman' in there. Only one that meant something...enough to risk—"

"You? Enough to risk *you?*" He placed his hands on her shoulders, stopping her from walking away. "There is no one like that, Angela. Don't you realize that by now?"

"Then who *is* she?" she asked angrily, facing him with burning tears welling up in her eyes. "And what was she doing with you?"

"She wasn't 'with me.' Not exactly, anyway."

"Adam!" she cried in frustration and pushed away from him. "Either explain this or leave."

"It's Patty," he replied. "She's here, with Brandon."

Brandon. Patty's son. The child Adam had thought was his own.

"Why?" Angela asked as she studied Adam's haunted expression. "What does she want?"

"She wants my help," he responded, releasing his hold on her and staring bleakly into her cautious, blue eyes.

Her heart sank. Patty would want Adam. She'd be a fool not to. "She wants *you,*" Angela corrected quietly. Of all the concerns she'd had about this relationship, it had never occurred to her to worry about Patty. Her teeth sank into her lower lip as she considered the possibilities. Maybe Patty wanted a future with some stability...a real home, maybe. Specifically, a *log* home. With Adam Dalton in residence. "So she can do that? She can just show up at your house as though she belongs there?"

"No," he said, but his adamant response did little to ease Angela's fears. "Brandon's father left her, she lost her job and she happened to find out where I live through my brother."

"Did he give her a key to your house? And did he hand her the bathrobe? Or did *you?*" she asked quietly, blinking back threatening tears.

"No," Adam answered with emphasis. "It's nothing like that. Patty is no threat to us."

"But she has Brandon. And probably a better hold on you than you know."

"He's not my son."

"That's what you say, but how do you feel when you see him now?"

He looked at her for a long, silent moment, and then shook his head. "I feel sorry for the boy. Patty hasn't given him much of a home." He reached out to touch Angela's cheek. "He just turned thirteen, and he needs a decent father figure in his life, but it's not going to be me."

Angela moved easily into his arms, burying her face in his shoulder. "I don't want to lose you, not even to Brandon. God forgive me, I know that sounds selfish probably to you and the Lord and everyone else."

Adam touched the soft hair at her temple. "You're not going to lose me."

She raised her head. "But Adam, she's at your home—"

"Listen to me," he began, "Patty found an extra house key I keep in the garage, so she and Brandon went inside while I was still at work. I had no idea they were there until I came home. She had showered and changed clothes before I got there, and Brandon was watching television. I was running a little later than usual, so I was surprised you weren't already there. Eventually, she got around to telling me about you coming to the door, and about the bathrobe and...I knew you'd be upset."

"Why should I be upset?" she exclaimed. "After all, it was just a beautiful woman wrapped in a bathrobe that I found inside the home of the man I love. I could be wrong, Adam, but my guess is that that little discovery would upset 99 percent of the female population."

"Think so, huh?" Adam asked quietly with an undeniable hint of amusement in his expression.

But Angela's crystal blue eyes lowered to the knit fabric of Adam's shirt as she fought the threatening sob rising in her throat. Should she say what she was thinking? "I don't want her staying with you. I don't want you going home to her tonight. If you're going home to anyone, it should be to *me*."

"Angela—" Adam gently placed a hand under her chin and raised her gaze to meet his gentle gray eyes "—I'm not going to touch Patty."

"But I don't even want you to *want* to touch her,"

she said, placing her hand over her heart as if to shield it, "and if she spends the night there—"

"You don't trust me much, do you?" he said, brushing his mouth tenderly against her crown.

"Not with a woman that looks like that," Angela admitted.

"Then how could I be trusted with a woman who looks like you?" he asked as his hands moved to tenderly touch both sides of her face.

A soft sigh of frustration escaped as she once again leaned her forehead against his shoulder. "Adam, don't. I just want Patty out of your house. Is that so wrong? I mean, couldn't she stay with your brother? Or someone else who is safely, happily married?" Angela looked up at him.

"She's already gone. I paid for a hotel room and gave them money for meals, gasoline...necessities." Adam kissed the crease of worry that knitted Angela's brows together. "Patty has both her parents and three brothers she can go to, and that's exactly what I told her. I've done my share for her. If I'm going to help anyone, it's going to be you."

Angela blinked. "What?" she asked quietly, thinking she had surely misunderstood him. "Help me?"

Adam wasn't sure what he'd said wrong, but from the look of disbelief that sparked in Angela's eyes, he knew it had been something significant. "You're a woman, alone, Angela, with three kids to raise."

"I don't need your help," she stated quietly, calmly, as her anger slowly mounted. "Is that what I am to you? Someone to help?" She pulled away from him, knowing she was probably angrier than she should be. But being lumped in with other ‘‘needy’’ females had always been a sore point with her. She’d managed things pretty well this far in life without much assistance from a man.

‘‘No,’’ he responded quickly. ‘‘It’s much more than that—you know it is.’’ He raised a hand to touch her face, but she backed away, folding her arms in front of her.

‘‘But what was it in the beginning? Did I start out as some sort of mission project?’’

‘‘Of course not.’’ Adam lowered his head and rubbed a hand over his face in frustration. How had this conversation gone so wrong? ‘‘It started because I was attracted to you, Angela. You’re so…easy to talk to and—’’

‘‘Needy?’’ she added, barely able to say the word without screaming it at him. Was that where all of this began? ‘‘I was the poor widow, or divorcee…or whatever it is I am.’’ She turned to walk away, put more distance between them—as if there wasn’t enough emotional distance between them already. ‘‘You thought—’’

‘‘I thought, ‘There’s a beautiful woman I want to get to know.’ ’’

‘‘You don’t need to tell me I’m beautiful just because I’ve seen your first wife. There’s no comparison. Patty is gorgeous. Don’t say—’’

‘‘Say what? That you’re beautiful? Is the truth always this hard for you to accept?’’ He searched her expression for some glimpse of the understanding he needed to see.

She shook her head, her dark hair moving softly around her face. The sadness deep within her eyes pierced Adam's heart. Had he become the source of that sorrow? He spanned the empty space between them, touching her shoulder gently, wanting her in his arms. How had he hurt her so when all he ever wanted was to hold her, love her?

"Adam, don't."

"Do you remember that night at the rec center? The Open House? You were envious of Tiffany. Her youth, her looks, whatever...and I wondered why. Why on earth would you be bothered by her? Or any other woman?" Strong, sure hands moved to her waist, preventing her from inching away. "Angie, you're everything I want."

"No, I'm not," she assured him. "I'm not needy enough for you to rescue, and not beautiful enough to hold your attention even now that I have it. Patty showing up today proved that."

"Patty has nothing to do with my love for you or how attractive you are." He hesitated. He hadn't wanted to tell her yet that he loved her. He'd wanted a more tender moment.

But Angela's sadness remained. *Love.* He'd never mentioned it before tonight. Did he mean it? Was he sure? She knew that any doubts she'd had about her feelings for him had vanished at Patty's arrival and at the thought of him in someone else's arms. But how did the presence of his former love affect him? "Don't say things you don't mean."

Adam studied her downcast expression silently for a moment. "What did Dan do that so destroyed your self-esteem?" he asked in the quietness. "Or was it the things he *didn't* do?"

She pulled away. "Dan doesn't have anything to do with this."

"He has everything to do with it," Adam countered. "He was the man in your life for more than a decade. Much of what you think of yourself has come from him."

He was right, Angela knew, although she was reluctant to admit it. "Our marriage wasn't a good one, but my not being beautiful didn't have much to do with it."

"Come with me," Adam said suddenly. He grasped her hand in his, leading her through the living room toward the back hallway. She was too startled by his actions to protest. He led her past the boys' bedroom and then Heather's room before he pushed open the door to the cluttered bathroom.

"Adam? Why are we going in here?" And why had she left panty hose and wet towels draped over the shower door? Because, she recalled, they weren't supposed to be here tonight. They were to have been at *his* place.

"Look," he stated, turning her toward the large rectangular mirror that hung over the vanity. He flipped on the light switch to the left of the glass. "Your hair is a gorgeous black-brown color I can hardly describe. You have the clearest, lightest blue eyes I've ever seen. And your face...." He paused, and the approval of what he saw so apparent in his steady gaze did nothing to alleviate the tension that had been building between them for weeks. Angela's breath caught audibly in her throat when Adam's warm palm and fingers touched her cheek. "How I love that face...."

Angela's eyes shifted in the mirror from her own features to Adam's profile: the firm set of his mouth, the gentle look in his eyes, the dark blond hair she knew would be soft against her fingertips. These feelings she had for him were unlike any she'd known. How could she find a way to explain them? She didn't want to be helped or rescued. She just wanted *him*. Forever.

Unless Patty was the catalyst. That was exactly how it had been with Dan Sanders. On the rebound from a former love, he'd pursued the lonely college girl Angela had been at nineteen, and got more than he bargained for: Nathan. Now here she was, with Adam. Did he have any of these feelings for her last night or the night before? And would he tomorrow? Or was she someone to want and need in lieu of what might have been? She raised her eyes to look cautiously into a storm of gray.

"Angie, I know it's difficult for you to trust, and I'm trying to give you time but—" he stopped, and his warm gaze traveled over her face "—we don't need to keep seeing each other for me to know that my feelings for you are serious. Very serious. I've known that for a long time."

"Lucky thing you found a woman you could help *and* feel serious about at the same time. That makes a tidier package, doesn't it?" Her words were sharp, but the questioning look she gave him made it clear that she wasn't sure of anything anymore. Least of all, him.

Adam didn't respond right away. The things he wanted to say, shouldn't be said. Not yet. He moved his hand, to her jawline, where a warm thumb caressed one corner of her mouth until Angela lowered her eyes to stare at the plum carpeting at her feet.

"You're right, you know," he said gently, "you don't need me. I'm the one who needs you." He paused. Should he say what he felt? "Angie, you said earlier that I'm the man you love. Did you mean that?"

She nodded, unable to answer without a fear of a sob.

"Then look at me," he said.

Angela raised watery eyes to see the warmth she knew she'd find in his—along with confidence, certainty, clarity. He was a man who knew exactly what he wanted. She'd always thought that about him, even when he didn't think it about himself.

"I don't need more time to know who I want. Do you?"

She shrugged a little, almost hopelessly. "I don't want to make a mistake."

"Our being together is no mistake." He spoke

gently, tenderly, and his heart pounded loudly within his chest. *God, I love this woman You've brought into my life. Don't let me lose her now,* he thought. *Not like this, not with inadequate words.*

"Adam..." she began before her resolve melted in the warmth of his touch. In an almost painful motion, she covered the strong hand that lay so gently against her cheek and pulled his hand away. And he did not resist her action, although it nearly broke his waiting heart. She was slipping a little farther away from him, and he didn't know what to do or say to repair whatever had gone wrong. Then Angela continued, "You could be with Patty right now. You know that as well as I do. But she hurt you before and she might hurt you again. So is that why you want me now? Because I'm safer? Is that why I seem beautiful and lovely and—"

"Angela?" His voice sharpened and his eyes flashed with anger and hurt at the accusation. "Do you think I would do that—use you like that?" Why hadn't he told her how pretty she was or how much he wanted her before now, when it seemed so shallow. And too little too late. Because she wouldn't have believed him then, either.

"I don't know," she stated honestly. With a quick turn, she put distance between them and stepped out of the narrow bathroom. "Why did Patty have to show up now?" Tears burned her eyes, but not in sadness. She was angry. At Patty, at Dan, at Adam, at men and their stupid rescue attempts. "I think you should go," she added quickly, thoughtlessly, as she walked back toward the living room. Her heart was thundering and the undeniable bond between them still threatened to overwhelm her. "Go—before this turns into something more than I can handle."

"Like what? A loving relationship with a man who wants you?" he asked, his voice deadly quiet. He'd thought this before, but hadn't wanted to say it to her so plainly. Now it seemed to be the one thing that needed to be said. "Are you still so affected by the fact that Dan left you for another woman?"

"No!" she replied, surprised at his remark.

"I'm sorry that he's dead, Angela, or at least, God help me, I'm trying to be. But he's not here for you to win back and redeem your self-worth."

Angela laughed, stunned by his comment. "Win him back? Do you think that's what I'd want to do?" Adam had no idea how off-course his thinking was. How could she explain to him how little she and Dan had come to mean to each other?

"Yes," Adam answered, "that's exactly what I think. And if Dan Sanders was too big a fool to realize what he had waiting for him at home, that was his own loss. I can't fix that for you. I'm not the guy who left." He paused. "At least, I wasn't until tonight."

"You're not leaving me," Angela reminded in quick response. "I'm the one who asked *you* to go. Remember?"

"Does it really matter so much?" he asked in a voice that was cold and distant. "The loss is the same for both of us, no matter who moves first." His angry gaze burned through her before he turned to walk out. He'd said all the wrong things, he knew. Anger had a way of doing that to him. He'd have turned around in a second if she'd called his name. She was all he wanted. Now. Always. But the door closed with a quiet click behind him, and he walked through the night air to his truck with his hands jammed into the pockets of his jacket.

Then an old thought crossed his mind. No. Angela wasn't all he wanted. Not at this particular moment. He got into the vehicle and slammed the door shut. Maybe it really was better, easier at least, to walk away now while there was still some dignity in it. Later would be worse. Adam closed his eyes momentarily against the cold, stinging temperature. More painful than right now? He doubted anything could top this.

Back inside the stillness of her apartment, Adam's name was called, but not for his hearing. The sound was muffled by the palm of Angela's hand as she covered her mouth to hold back the accompanying sob. She hadn't wanted it to end. She hadn't meant to be so hurtful, to send him away—probably to Patty and Brandon. She'd only meant to protect her own heart. But now, for the first time, she saw clearly that it was no longer hers to protect. It belonged to the man who'd just walked out that door.

''Mom, it's me.'' Angela spoke softly into the telephone receiver.

"Hello, dear. I didn't expect to hear from you quite so soon. Is everything all right?"

Angela hesitated. "Not exactly," she replied with a heartsick laugh. "Mom, Adam and I—Adam is gone."

"Gone," Grace Granston repeated. "Gone? I don't understand—"

"We had a huge argument. He left here incredibly angry with me," Angela said.

"Why? What happened?"

"I don't know. I guess he's just not quite as perfect as he seems."

"No one ever is," Grace commented.

"No, I suppose not." Angela sighed. "How are the kids?"

"Fine. David just got here a short time ago. John's family kept him with them for dinner, and then brought him here." Grace waited a moment before speaking again. "Do you want to talk about this?"

"Maybe later, Mom. Not right now." Angela paused. "Does Nathan seem okay? I had a really difficult discussion with him today."

"He's been quieter than usual. He and Grandpa are downstairs playing video games, as you might have guessed."

"Okay. I'll be over to get them soon."

"Angela, if you need some time—to be alone or to speak with Adam—they could stay longer."

"No, Mom, but thanks for asking. I can't work this out with Adam. Not now. We're both too upset. I'm going to change clothes, and I'll see you soon."

"All right. We'll be watching for you, but take a little time for yourself first. Drink a cup of tea or take a long, hot shower...something soothing."

"Thanks, Mom. Maybe I will." But as Angela said goodbye, she wondered if she would ever again be able to shower without thinking of a partially dry, partially dressed Patty standing in Adam's doorway.

"Mom!" Heather exclaimed when Angela quietly entered the family room of the Granston home about an hour later. "We didn't hear you at the door."

"I used my key so no one would need to come running upstairs to let me in." She hugged her daughter just as one of Grace's cats ran up to her and rubbed its back against Angela's ankles. Then she looked across the room at the boys, where they sat engrossed in a video game. "Hey, guys. We gotta go. It's getting late."

"Five minutes? Please, Mom?" David begged. "Just let me move up one more level."

"Five minutes. Then out to the van." She responded to David's pleas, but studied Nathan's profile as he concentrated on the screen in front of him. Her eldest child didn't acknowledge her presence.

Ed Granston looked over at his daughter. "Sweatpants and a T-shirt? Where did you and Adam go tonight? Out to pick pumpkins?"

"Grandpa! I'm the one who picked pumpkins today. On the field trip. Remember?" reminded Heather.

Angela patted her little girl's dark curls. "I

changed before I came to pick up the kids. Adam and I didn't go anywhere tonight,'' she answered, hoping she didn't seem noticeably evasive. That would bring more questions from the father who didn't miss much of what was happening in his children's lives. ''Heather, hon, get your sweater and whatever you brought with you. I'm going to the kitchen with Grandma for a few minutes.''

Grace followed Angela's cue and headed toward what limited privacy they would have in a house with six people.

''Adam's ex-wife came to town today,'' Angela explained quietly when they entered the room decorated with attractive baskets and strawberry designs.

''The one with the child?'' Grace's eyebrows raised in obvious concern.

''Yes. The boy is about Nathan's age, and Patty…well, she's so pretty and young looking—let's just say she's gorgeous. The drop-dead kind, if you know what I mean.''

''Did Adam introduce you?'' Grace asked as she sat down at the table.

''No. She was at his house when I went over there for dinner. He'd given me a key so I could let myself in if I arrived before he did. So the front door opened, and there she stood, fresh from a shower and wrapped in a big robe—probably Adam's.'' Angela sank onto a kitchen chair and ran her fingers around the edge of a placemat the color of strawberries. ''Just seeing her was….'' Angela searched for the right word.

"Was...what? Enough to destroy what little self-confidence you've acquired recently?"

"You know me too well," Angela replied.

"I know you well enough to realize you think practically every woman you encounter is better looking than you. And usually smarter, too, and more spiritual and a better mother—"

"Okay, okay. I get your point, Mom," she answered. "But with Patty, it's not something I'm imagining. Give me some credit here. I do have good eyesight, you know."

"Good enough to notice whether Adam was there, too? At home, with Patty and his robe?"

"As it turned out, Adam wasn't there. Patty and Brandon had let themselves in with an extra key she'd found in the garage. They were there, unannounced, waiting on him when he returned home from the center this evening." Angela shook her head, thinking how ridiculous the situation sounded. "So after my encounter with her, I went home. It wasn't long until Adam came to my apartment to explain."

"I should hope so!" Grace exclaimed. "He certainly had some explaining to do."

"But he did just that. Explained away her unexpected appearance, his brother giving her Adam's address, the key in the garage, her recent divorce and unemployment...he had an explanation for everything."

"Is she still there? Staying with him?"

Angela shook her head. "No. He gave them money

for a hotel room and necessities. They're on their way to her family's home, wherever that is."

"So, Patty and her son are gone. How did Adam react to seeing the boy again?" Grace asked.

"I think it was difficult. He knows the child needs a father, but he said it couldn't be him."

Grace smiled. "So he had the answers you needed to hear. She's gone. Nothing happened. And you're still mad at Adam?" She looked thoughtful. "Why? If you don't mind my asking."

"Because now, all of a sudden, Adam wants me. He thinks I'm beautiful and lovely and—"

"And that made you angry?" Grace asked, a dark frown on her face.

"Yes!" Angela exclaimed, then lowered her voice. "It all has to do with Patty. *She's* the one who's beautiful and lovely."

Grace's frown deepened. "But he said those things to you, Angela, not to Patty. Right?"

"Yes. He couldn't have Patty, so he came to me."

"Couldn't have Patty? I think he could have had Patty any way he wanted her. I'm sure Adam knows that, too. But he sent her away. How can you be mad at him?"

"He sent her away because she'd hurt him once, and he knew it could happen again. So suddenly, I look pretty good to him, when all I really am is a safer bet."

"You've been dating him for weeks. You obviously 'looked pretty good' to him long before tonight."

"Well, apparently I looked especially good tonight because tonight it was me he wanted," Angela replied, trying to keep her voice down to a level that the children couldn't hear.

"Mom, we're ready. We're goin' on out," David called from the hallway where the three were putting on their jackets.

Angela stood up, looking in the direction of their voices. "Anyway, he was very angry when he left my apartment, and I was, too." She turned to leave the kitchen.

Grace reached out and caught Angela's arm before she could walk through the doorway. "Are you telling me you don't have similar feelings toward him?" she asked quietly, as the front door opened and the children headed outside.

Angela stopped and looked into her mother's inquisitive brown eyes. "No, Mom. I have those same feelings, but I want him forever, and I want him to want me for whom I am—not because I'm more trustworthy than Patty."

Grace nodded. "I understand, and I agree with your view entirely, but it might be helpful if you told him how you feel. Don't make him guess. Tell him what you want."

Angela laughed softly. "Right, Mom. What do you think I should do? Tell him I want to marry him?"

"It would be a good place to start." Grace patted Angela's arm before releasing her. "And when you discuss this with Adam, remember it's Adam you're talking to. Not Dan."

Dan. Angela suddenly recalled that that was exactly who she had thought of before and during their argument. Maybe she hadn't been fair to Adam. "Thanks, Mom." She gave her mother a hug and a kiss on the cheek. "See you later."

Then Angela and the children headed home. The kids all fell asleep during the ride to the apartment, allowing Angela freedom to run over and over in her mind the argument she'd had with Adam that evening. Could she have misunderstood? Had Patty reminded her too much about Dan and the past for her to have been objective where Adam was concerned? Should she call him? Tell him her feelings? Wait for an apology, or offer one of her own? She needed time to sort through her thoughts. Angela sighed as she made the last turn toward home. Had Adam asked for less than she had assumed? Or more?

Chapter Eleven

He picked up the ringing phone. ‘‘Rec Center. Adam Dalton speaking.’’

‘‘Adam,’’ she started, then stopped.

He could hardly believe it was her. ‘‘Angela?’’ It seemed as if it had been such a long time since he'd spoken with her. And their last words had been so harsh.

‘‘I was wondering…could you get away for lunch? With me?’’ she asked.

‘‘Hold on a minute.’’ There was silence while he apparently checked his schedule. ‘‘I could get out of here around 12:30.’’

‘‘That would be good,’’ she responded and closed her eyes momentarily in relief. This wouldn't be easy, but she'd made up her mind. Now she could get it over with—soon.

Adam interrupted her thoughts. ‘‘I'll pick you up at—’’

"No, I'll pick *you* up," she corrected. "I'll be by to get you at 12:30. See you then." She hung up without waiting for his goodbye.

"Hi," she said, smiling a little as he reached to open the door of her van and slide into the passenger seat. But there was no smile waiting for her in return.

"You haven't answered my calls for a week," he stated rather matter-of-factly. "Are you sure you want to do this?"

The gray eyes that viewed her seemed cautious. Unfamiliar. Angela cleared her throat nervously as she nodded her head and returned her attention to driving.

"I thought we might go to the park, if that sounds okay. I stopped at a restaurant and picked up a couple of chicken sandwiches and two iced teas."

"The park would be fine if it's private. We have plenty to talk about." Adam had even more to discuss than Angela suspected. He was determined to tell her about his past, and his present and future—the future he hoped she might still want to share.

Within ten awkward minutes, they arrived at the spot Angela remembered from her last picnic with the children. Feeling the not-quite-warm breeze of autumn, she reached for a sweater on the seat behind her, and Adam picked up the lunch she had brought. "See that spot right there?" She nodded toward a huge oak tree offering leaves in deep fall hues. "I have this old tablecloth the kids and I sit on when we come here." She gathered it up from the rear of the van and joined Adam by the place she'd suggested to spread the cloth on the ground. Then they sat down. But no one reached for the sandwiches.

"Do you need to be back at the office soon?" Adam asked in what Angela took as an attempt at casual conversation rather than any real interest in her schedule.

"No, actually, I don't. I have a couple of hours of comp time I'm using to run errands, eat lunch...and talk with you."

Adam turned his head slightly, studying her expression. And all Angela could think of was how much she'd missed him during the long, miserable week she'd endured. How was she going to tell him all she had to say?

But Adam spoke first. "Angela, about what I said the other night—"

"Don't." She raised her hand to silence him. "Don't apologize for feeling the very same things for me that I feel for you." She looked fully into his eyes and knew from his immediate frown that he had not been certain of her feelings for him; she hadn't let him be certain because she hadn't been sure of those feelings, either. Until Patty showed up. "You seem to be quicker than I am to say what you think and how you feel. It was no different the other night."

Adam shook his head. "You say more than you realize with those eyes," he commented. "I'd never apologize for the way I feel about you, but I am sorry for the way I expressed it. 'Want' was not the word to use in telling you that I hope for a future with you.

I just didn't think about how it might have sounded at that time, especially after the incident with Patty."

"Oh, Adam, I was so upset that day," she responded in a gush of words and feelings. "I'd had such a horrible afternoon with Nathan, and I needed to talk to you about it. Then at your front door I encountered Patty, of whom I am still insanely jealous."

"Don't be. You're the woman I'm in love with."

"But you hadn't mentioned love until *she* showed up," Angela reminded, glancing down at her skirt rather than meeting his gaze. "I didn't want your reaction to Patty sending you into my arms."

"Why would you even think such a thing?" he asked. "Don't you know how I feel about you?"

She nodded her head and looked up at him. "I think I do now," she answered, touching his jawline with her fingertips.

Adam reached up, covering Angela's slender hand with his own. The lines etched at the corners of his eyes deepened a little as the beginning of a smile teased his mouth. "Now and always. I love you, Angie."

She sighed softly. "I wish you had said it so plainly that night. Adam, how could things get so mixed up?"

"I don't know, but sometimes they do." He paused for a moment, remembering something she'd said earlier. "What about you and Nathan? Did you get things worked out with him?" He watched her pull away from him to reach for an iced tea.

"I think so. As much as possible," she answered, thinking back to that afternoon. "I had to tell him some things about his dad...and me...and our marriage." She paused, remembering her son's angry response and the tears and self-doubt that followed. "Dealing with Nathan's questions, seeing Patty in your home, then the things that happened between us that night—all of it made me think of parts of my life you know nothing about."

"Then tell me," he pleaded. "I want you, Angie...everything about you, everything that comes with you."

"I want that, too," she answered, thankful for tender words that eased the tension. "After Dan left me, I didn't think I would want another man in my life. *Ever.* Then you came along and made me 'feel' again." She sighed. "I'd learned how to not do that, you know. And I was pretty good at it. But now, I'm not even sure how I'm supposed to act anymore. I've never *felt* this way until now...until you." She lowered her gaze to the ground. "I've never really been in love."

Adam's hand touched her chin, gently bringing her gaze up to meet his questioning eyes. "But," he began quietly, "how can that be—"

"I was pregnant when I married Dan," Angela stated bluntly, cutting off Adam's words and clearly surprising him with her candidness. "I'll bet you wouldn't have guessed that about me, would you?" She raised a hand to shield her eyes from a temporary glare of the sun as she looked away from him. "My mother has already asked me if I'm sleeping with you. Never mind the fact that I'm thirty-two years old, a mother of three and a school principal. She still felt the need to inquire.'' She set down the iced tea.

''I would have thought your mom might show more respect for you than to ask something so personal.''

Angela shook her head. ''It's not lack of respect as much as it is a parent frightened of what lies ahead of her child. You know what I mean? It's as though she's still trying to be a good parent to the kid I was then in hopes of keeping me from making 'shipwreck' of my life again, as she called it.''

''Did you remind her that your values are different from what they used to be? That you're trying to live a Christian life-style?''

''That's part of the problem,'' she admitted reluctantly. ''Back then, I'd been a Christian for years. I was in a Christian college, attending church regularly, living life the way I think it should be lived. I started drifting away from all of that after something happened that changed everything.''

Adam waited as she searched for the right words. She'd run through this a hundred times in her mind, thinking it would make the discussion easier. It didn't.

''You see, back then my brother Rob had been a Christian longer than I had, and we went to the same school, Trinity College. But he was a couple of years ahead of me. His best friend, Nick Alsmore, was his roommate and Nicky was a Christian, too—and a very good friend of our family. He and Rob were ready to graduate when Nick was killed in a car accident. After that, Rob basically gave up on God."

"Rob? Your brother, the pastor?" Adam asked.

"Yes, that's him. He was a long time coming back to the Lord after Nick's death. About ten years, actually. We had been very close until the accident. Then suddenly, it was as though he was a different person. He didn't have anything to do with church anymore, and I think he knew I didn't belong with his new friends or his new life-style. I guess he protected me from that by leaving me out. But I felt very alone. Loving God...even just being a Christian...it suddenly seemed difficult to continue on with things Rob no longer valued. His opinion had always meant more to me than probably anyone else's ever had." She glanced at Adam and saw understanding in his eyes.

"Angela, I'm sure that was a difficult time in your life," Adam offered, all the while thinking of how much harder *his* admission would be for her to accept than anything she had to say to him today. "You don't need to explain."

"Yes, I do." She smiled as she looked at the man who listened patiently to her words. "It's part of who I am."

"Who you *were*," he corrected.

"True," she laughed lightly, lowering her gaze to the warm hand resting close by hers and wishing he would touch her again. "I'm not a kid anymore, not a college student." Then a new seriousness entered her voice. "...not lonely, needy, frightened...or stupid."

"Of the many things you may be, stupid is not among them," Adam said quietly.

She shrugged. "Not anymore, at least. So, as the story goes, I met Dan, who had no interest whatsoever in God. He was at a Christian college because his parents had made it clear to him that he could go to any college he chose, but that if he wanted *them* to pay for it, he would go to Trinity, his father's alma mater." Angela took another drink. "I'm talking so much my throat is getting dry."

Adam smiled. "Do you want to eat your sandwich and finish talking later?"

"No. I'd rather get this over with." She held the foam cup in her hand and fiddled nervously with the straw. "So I started dating Dan. That was my decision, *my* mistake. But Rob, even to this day, blames himself for that relationship."

"Because if he'd been watching out for you, he wouldn't have let you get involved with Dan?"

Angela frowned. "How'd you know?"

"I've seen your boys watch over Heather. I think that's how they'd feel about it, too, if something like that happened to her."

"Oh, no," Angela moaned softly. "I can't even think about Heather in that situation. I want her to have what I've found with—" she stopped, suddenly feeling almost shy "—with you," she finished.

Adam nodded. "I want *us* to have what you've found with me, too, Angela."

"So do I," she agreed with a smile. "But I need to tell you more."

"I know, go ahead."

She paused momentarily, wishing she had taken two aspirin before she'd left home. This was every bit as difficult as she'd suspected it would be. Maybe more so. "Dan had recently broken up with a long-time girlfriend after she met someone new. And there *I* was...so he took an interest in me. Then, I don't know what happened exactly. He said he loved me, and wanted to marry me. I guess I believed him. Maybe I thought I loved him, too. It doesn't matter now. It was still no excuse for what happened. We hadn't been seeing each other any time at all when I became pregnant. And there I was, still practically a kid myself...going to have a baby with some guy I barely knew."

"And your parents? They probably took the news badly." Adam could only imagine what that news must have done to Grace and Ed Granston.

Angela grimaced. "Badly, but differently," she explained. "Dad, more or less, wanted to kill Dan if he wouldn't marry me, and Mom didn't want me to get married. She thought I should live at home, have the baby and finish school."

"She must have been perceptive enough to know Dan wouldn't make you happy. Not for a lifetime."

"That's it, basically," Angela replied with a sad smile. "Mom knows me pretty well. She knew I'd stay with him regardless of how I felt. She said I was stubborn and determined enough that if I committed my life to Dan in marriage, I'd be stuck there forever. Unhappily ever after."

Adam looked away. *"Unhappily ever after." Lord, don't let me do that to her, too.* "So that's pretty much what happened?"

Angela nodded. "Almost. We got married because I wanted to try to somehow make things right, and he knew his parents would cut off the college money if he refused to live up to his responsibilities. So we married in the spring, had Nathan at the end of the summer, and tried to make something of a normal life for ourselves." She stopped talking for a moment, trying to recall what else she had wanted to explain. "I had the distinction of being the first woman in our family to 'have to get married' for as far back as anyone can recall, and, believe me, I tried very hard to 'recall' such an incident. But I couldn't. And I was determined not to be the first divorce, too. That was more distinction than I wanted. So I finished school with Mom and Dad's help, got a teaching job, made more money than Dan, looked after practically everything you can imagine on the home front, including car repairs, maintaining health insurance, paying bills—everything."

"And Dan?"

"He did mostly what he wanted—drank too much, had his friends to hang around with."

Drank too much? Had he heard her correctly? For Adam, it seemed like time stood still as he considered her words—what they meant, what they'd mean in the days to come. "You've never mentioned the drinking."

Angela shrugged. "It's not something I talk about much, now or even during our marriage. I suppose it was the typical 'family secret' kind of thing. The only people I've really opened up to have been the women in a support group I used to belong to for families of alcoholics. When Dan left us to start divorce proceedings, I stopped being part of that group." She smiled. "It felt so good, Adam, to be away from it all, to actually put it behind me and go on. You can't imagine how that felt."

Yes, Adam could imagine that. Especially Angela's newfound sense of freedom. And he was about to take that feeling away from her. *Oh, Lord, should I tell her this now? Now?* "Angela—"

"Adam—"

They'd spoken each other's name at exactly the same moment, and then laughed a little in awkwardness.

"Let me talk first," she said, not wanting to wait another moment to be certain of his intentions. "Did you mean what you said? That you want me, all that comes with me?" She caught her lower lip between her teeth as she awaited his reply.

"Yes," he answered honestly. *But Lord, You know she may not want all that comes with* me. "Angela—"

"Three kids? Do you realize what you're saying? What you're committing to?"

"Yes," he answered. But do you? he thought. Acceptance of him, just as he was. That's how the Lord had received him years ago, and that's what he needed from Angela now and in all the days to come. "I love you, Angie—"

"I love you, too, Adam. I will for the rest of my life," she proclaimed. And with an uneasy boldness, she leaned forward, touching Adam's mouth in a brief, fleeting movement.

He barely kissed her back. "Angela, how did you—why did you stay married?" She'd been through so much. Did he dare hope that she would take a chance now? With him?

"We didn't talk about staying married. It just happened. Probably because he loved the kids too much to leave," she said, then paused. "You know, he wasn't a good father to them in most ways, but sometimes I saw him really try. I think that's what made me care about him more as the years went by. I wanted him to change. For a while, I thought maybe he would. But he couldn't give it up. He couldn't stay sober long enough to make things work. Then, several months before he died, he met Sylvia—his kindred spirit, I guess you could say. Anyway, he filed for divorce from me because he wanted a life with her." She set the iced tea down on the blanket. "I was glad he found someone else, glad he wanted out. My freedom was such a pleasant surprise." She looked up at Adam again, trying to judge his reaction. "Sounds awful of me, doesn't it?"

"Sounds honest." Adam touched the soft, dark strands of hair resting against Angela's shoulder. A glimpse of hurt shone in her eyes from bitter memories. What did that leave Adam to do? Hurt her more?

"You probably think I was a terrible wife to him, but I really wasn't."

"I wouldn't think—"

"You'd have every right to assume that about me, but you'd be wrong if you did. I really tried to make it work. And as the years passed, I cared about him very much. It was never what it should have been. Not from day one. But I tried. Especially in the early years. If he hadn't been an alcoholic, we'd have had a better chance."

"I wish you'd told me sooner. About the drinking, I mean," Adam said slowly. *Dear God, I wish she had mentioned it,* he thought frantically. *I'd have stayed away from her entirely if I'd known.*

"I guess I don't talk much about Dan or our marriage or any of it anymore. He's gone now, and I am very careful of what I say in front of the kids. They loved their father. I don't want to be disrespectful to his memory." With a quiet sigh, she continued, "But the drinking was very hard on them. Occasionally, he wouldn't come home at night, and we wouldn't know where he was. I got used to it, but they couldn't."

"Didn't he try to quit? I mean, Angela, there are counselors and programs—"

"I know," Angela interrupted. "He tried several times, but it never lasted long." She shrugged. "After a while, I gave up hoping."

Adam's heart sank even deeper. How could he tell

her this? She'd be terrified of a future with him if she knew about his past. But then he remembered one bright spot of hope. She had stayed with Dan to the end rather than run away from the problems. Would she have that kind of endurance again? Adam moved closer and brushed her temple with a tentative kiss. "But you stayed with him through it all?"

"Yes," she responded, "if there hadn't been another woman, I would have stayed—forever." She stared down at her left hand, void of rings. "I was married a long time, Adam. I never dreamed I'd have a second chance...that I'd have you...that I'd ever feel this way."

The look of concern that tightened his expression relaxed a little as he considered how much he loved this woman beside him. He knew she had no idea what he was going to ask of her. A lifetime, yes—but lived one day at a time. There were no doubts in her mind. Only certainty and love could be read in her look, and the happiness of today. Could he take that away from her?

Angela moved into his embrace as if she'd been made to fit there, and Adam held her close. She felt so warm and smelled wonderful with some soft summer scent of perfume. And it had been such a long time since he'd held her like this. But his heart pounded with the truth. "Angie...," he began.

She lifted her head to look into his eyes. "This is one of the happiest days of my life," she said, with a look filled with the love and trust that Adam knew he didn't deserve. If he told her now—ruined this moment for her—would she hate him for that?

"I love you, Adam." Angela spoke gentle words to his aching heart.

"And I love you, Angie," he responded, hating himself for his secrecy. But not enough to give it up. Not today. He couldn't break her heart, here and now, when he had just offered her the future.

With a new sense of belonging, Angela raised up, brushing Adam's mouth in a light, uncertain movement. But his arms slowly encircled her, pulling her closer, deeper into the warm kiss they both wanted. And Angela knew she could have spent a lifetime with him, right there, beneath the outstretched arms of that beautiful tree.

But time was slipping away. They'd been talking for almost two hours and she needed to pick up the children at school. Slowly, reluctantly, she eased from his arms. "Adam, we should leave."

Leave here and get back to reality, he thought briefly. He'd let her fall in love with him, let her think she knew the man she was committing her life to. If only he'd known about the part drinking had played in her marriage.... He'd have stayed away from her from the beginning.

"You probably need to pick up the kids," he said, rather than telling her what she needed to be told.

"Yes, and the two of us out here kissing like this—I mean, at our age? In the afternoon, at a park? Even if we were already married, a public display like this is almost indecent.'' She smiled in response to her own teasing words.

He smiled in return. ''I suppose you're right. Especially with you being a school principal. You could get expelled for behavior like this.''

''I think 'fired' is the word you're looking for. C'mon,'' she said, standing up and extending a hand toward Adam.

He stood up and took her hands in his. Then he kissed her again in an exchange that was gentle and much too brief. ''Adam?'' she complained.

''You're the one who said it was time to go.'' He squeezed her hand. ''Come on. You need to get back to school and I need to get in touch with Tiffany before she sends out a search party.'' He brushed off his brown corduroy slacks. ''I haven't taken a lunch break this long since I started working there.''

Angela reached for their drinks, as Adam picked up their now-cold food and the cloth from the ground.

''We forgot to eat our lunch,'' Adam commented as he placed the items inside her van. ''Hungry?'' he asked, opening the door for her to climb into the driver's seat.

''Starving, as usual. Let's get fresh sandwiches at a drive-through on the way back.''

He nodded. ''And stop at a pay phone so I can call in to explain why I won't be back for a while.'' He got into the van and shut his door. ''I'll ride to school with you to get the children.''

''They'll be so glad to see you. They've missed you.''

Adam smiled at her, studying the light in those blue eyes he loved. She'd want to tell the children their plans for the future. And her parents. He looked away from her to stare out the window. That might not be so bad. The closer they moved to actually marrying, the further she would be from wanting out later. Maybe.

"So," she added with a glance in his direction. "Let's have lunch."

"Grandma! Grandma! They're getting married!" Heather announced gleefully as they pulled into the long driveway to the Granston home and found Grace outside raking crunchy leaves into piles.

"What?" Grace asked when she looked up to see several members of her family arriving for an unexpected visit. "Married?"

The children were out of the van before Angela or Adam had a chance to unbuckle their seat belts.

"Mom and Adam are getting married," David explained to his grandmother, who was pulling off her garden gloves. "Soon!" he added with a wide grin. And Grace hugged him.

"It's about time," she remarked with a wide grin of her own. "What took you so long?" she asked when Adam and Angela finally joined her on the front lawn.

"I should have asked her weeks ago," Adam said. And at the same time, he knew he'd asked her too soon for her own good.

Angela gave him a sideways glance. "So soon?"

His arm slipped around her waist, drawing her close to his side. "Yes. You're everything I want in this life, Angie." His words were for all who listened, but his eyes, darkened with emotion, spoke only to her.

"Welcome to the family, Adam Dalton." Grace moved to kiss Adam's cheek and give a fierce hug to her daughter. "I wish you both much happiness. Kids, go find your granddad and tell him your mother has news that is a blessing to us in our old age."

Angela shook her head and sighed. "Honestly, Mother. You're only in your fifties."

Grace laughed and shooed the children off in search of their grandfather. "I'm so happy for both of you," she reiterated and hugged them simultaneously. "I couldn't be any happier with your choice," she said to Angela directly. "Or yours," she added, glancing again at Adam.

"Neither could I," Adam replied with a broad smile.

"I think I'll go help them find Dad," Angela said, and looked up at Adam. "Want to come with me?"

He shook his head. "Go ahead. I'll catch up in a minute."

Angela turned and started toward the house, pulling her bulky sweater close around her. Adam watched her walk away. Then he looked at her mother. "I'll take good care of her, Grace. And the kids."

"I know that. There's no need to even say it," she answered, shifting the rake from one hand to the other.

"Yes, there is," he replied. "She's been through a lot. I didn't know until today that Dan was an alcoholic."

Grace nodded and then sighed. Audibly. "She's seen some difficult days—years, actually. But with the Lord's help, she got through it okay. She wasn't with him because of love, you know."

Adam nodded. "She explained it to me earlier today. Do you think if Dan had sobered up—permanently—they could have worked it out?"

Grace thought for a moment before answering. "Possibly, if she could have believed he was really done with the drinking." Then she studied Adam's profile as he looked back in the direction Angela had taken. "Why? Does it matter?"

"It might," he responded, sliding his hands into the pockets of his dark slacks. He cleared his throat. "When I was in college, it was the accepted thing to drink a lot. For most of us, it wasn't a problem, but...." Then his words died out as he turned a solemn gaze on his future mother-in-law.

Grace closed her eyes and lowered her head to lean her forehead against the rake. "Oh, Adam, don't tell me—"

He nodded his head, just barely, but enough to confirm her suspicions. "I didn't have much of a chance to escape it. Both of my parents were alcoholics. They died very young because of it."

"Oh, Lord, help us out of this one," she remarked before looking back at Adam's guarded expression. "And Angela has no idea?"

"I couldn't tell her. Not today. I want to marry her, Grace. I want to have a child with her, have a *life* with her. And I won't have a chance if she finds this out now."

"You *must* tell her," Grace stated flatly. "If you don't, I will. I won't allow her to marry you without knowledge of this."

"I know. That's why I told you this now. It obligates *me* to tell her before the wedding. I don't want her hearing it from you."

"Don't *make* her hear this from me, Adam. It would be unforgivable if it doesn't come from you directly."

"I'll tell her," he responded and lowered his head to look at the pile of leaves nearby. "But not today."

Grace reached out a hand to touch his arm. "She loves you. She trusts you."

"Not enough for this news, she doesn't," he said with a sad smile. "I don't think she even trusts God enough to see us through this."

"We'll pray about that. She has a lot of faith in the Lord. He's seen her through so much. If she can feel that your union is in His will—not just what the two of you want—she can handle this. Mostly, with Angela, it's herself she doesn't trust. Her decisions, her choices in life...she lacks the self-confidence she needs to get through this easily. Give her some time, show her she can trust you," Grace said. "She can, can't she?"

"Yes, she can," he promised in a low voice.

"This problem...it's something you have control over now?" she asked.

"I haven't had a drink since I let God into my life over seven years ago. We'll be okay with it, Grace. It won't hurt Angela or the children," he assured her. "I wouldn't marry her if I thought it would."

There was silence for a moment between them, and then they saw Heather running across the yard.

"We'll all be trusting you on this one, Adam," Grace said as she watched her granddaughter coming toward her. Then Heather suddenly changed her course and headed into Adam's arms, bringing a smile and plenty of girlish giggling with her.

"Whoa! I almost didn't see that coming," he told the laughing child he now held in his arms. "You've gotta warn me so I can be ready to catch you next time." Sadness suddenly overwhelmed him as he considered how much he had come to love Angela's children. *Lord, let there be a next time with this child. A whole lifetime of them.*

"Looks like Angela went inside," Grace remarked. A light had come on in the kitchen of her house and her daughter was standing by the window where a calico cat slept, pressed against the window screen. "Maybe Micah is awake from her nap. I'm sure Angela will want to talk with her."

"How wonderful!" Micah responded excitedly to Angela's news of her upcoming marriage. "I'm so happy for you!" She lowered herself slowly, carefully onto the kitchen chair. "Sorry I can't run across the room to hug you, but I need to sit down.'' She sighed, mostly from weariness. ''So when will the wedding be?''

''I don't know. Thanksgiving, maybe?'' Angela replied. ''You and Rob will be up here for the holiday, anyway. It would be convenient—and soon.'' Angela glanced through the window at Adam, where he stood talking with her mother, and her heart flooded with joy. ''Just the sight of him....'' Her statement trailed off; it was difficult to find words for the contentment Adam had brought into her life.

''Wow, that sounds like love,'' Micah said, a hint of teasing in her tone.

Angela grinned when she was able to say, completely without jealousy, ''You should know. You've been there.''

''I'm still there,'' Micah replied quickly. ''And you'd better take a good look at me—all of me—because this is exactly where you could end up.''

''Could be,'' Angela agreed. Having Adam's child. It certainly wasn't the first time she'd thought of the possibility.

''And you'll be happier than I am because at least you'll know what you're doing. Two babies—Angela, what on earth am I going to do with two of them?'' Micah moaned. ''I don't even know how to handle one.''

Angela looked across the table at her sister-in-law and friend whose expression was suddenly one of utter hopelessness. What words of comfort could she find that would be meaningful? ''We'll help you. I'm sure Mother will want to be there when you come home from the hospital with the babies. And Rob will be with you. It's not like you're going into this all alone. The Lord knows what you're going through. He'll help you then just as He's done in the past."

"The best thing the Lord could do for me is to miraculously fill my heart and soul with a huge dose of maternal instinct. Apparently, I wasn't in line when He was handing that out." Micah's words were sharper than Angela had ever heard her speak, and she knew her anguish ran deep.

Angela rose from her chair and walked to Micah's side, putting a gentle hand on her friend's shoulder. Micah reached up, touching Angela's reassuring hand. "I'm so scared," she admitted. "I don't think I can handle this. I mean, the pregnancy, childbirth...that all seems easy compared to what must lie ahead. I wouldn't be as terrified if I were only dealing with one—but two? How am I going to live up to this?"

Angela crouched and looked up into Micah's sorrowful face, seeing the despair in her expression. "Take this one day at a time. Pregnancy, first. Raising babies, second. It will be okay—you'll see. It seems overwhelming now, but once you have them...."

"They don't come with instructions," she said with a sad laugh. "And I didn't learn those things growing up. I didn't even play with dolls much when I was a child. I preferred coloring, painting, even toy animals more! The only diapers I've ever changed have been Hope's girls', and I've never burped a baby. There are basic things I need to know!"

"You can do them," Angela responded emphatically. "When you get through most of these things the first time, you'll know how to do it. I realize I don't live close enough to help you very much, physically, unless I come on the weekends, but if you need to talk, call me. Anytime. Day or night. I'll help you in any way I can."

"No, I'm not going to bother you," Micah answered as a tear trickled down her cheek. "You and Adam will be newlyweds. I'm not going to intrude on your life that way."

"I want you to," Angela assured her. "I love you, Micah, and if I can help you in some way, I want to do that. And you've got to remember you'll have Rob. He's always been good with my kids and Eric's. He can change diapers and do a million other things that will help you. But you must accept the help that's offered—whether it's from me, Rob, Mom, Hope or whomever. Don't let yourself think that you're in this alone. That thought by itself can cause panic."

"*That* I already know," Micah said wryly. She wiped away the tears that had slowly found their way down her face. "Pray for me, okay?"

"Absolutely," Angela said. "But I want you to listen to what I'm saying and take my advice. Find someone—either at your church or in your neighborhood—who has a child close to the age of your babies, and become friends with her. The sooner you do that—have someone to share with, commiserate with, whatever—the better for both of you. When Nathan was born, I was still in school and Mom helped me a lot, so it went pretty smoothly. When David came along, however, we had recently moved into an apartment on the north side and I didn't know anyone in the area. That kind of isolation isn't emotionally healthy for you or the babies. You need someone to connect with, someone to spend time with. Go out to lunch, take the kids to the playground, go shopping together, trade baby-sitting, whatever. And I don't mean you need to spend a lot of money doing things together. It would be enough just to go back and forth to each other's homes during the week to drink coffee, watch the kids together and *talk*. Believe me, everyone will be happier that way. Especially you."

Micah nodded her head. "There are two other pregnant women in our church right now. One of them I know pretty well."

"Good. Try to develop a friendship that can benefit both of you. And don't forget Rob. Take time for him. Hire a baby-sitter and give yourself an evening alone together every now and then. Even a good marriage can sometimes get lost in the shuffle of parenthood."

"Did yours?" Micah asked softly, sadly.

"No," Angela answered truthfully. "It was lost before it ever began. Dan told me he started drinking when he was a teenager and, since then, he couldn't stop. I think all hope for our marriage was sacrificed somewhere back there in his bad choices."

Micah nodded. "But the Lord is giving you this second chance. I know you and Adam will be happy together." She glanced out the window framed by white curtains bordered with bright strawberry print. "He seems to get along fine with Grace and Heather. They're all standing out there talking among the leaves. The sky is so gray and cloudy. Looks like it might rain." She turned back to Angela. "You know, Grace is a wonderful mother-in-law. She's there when you need her—"

"...and not, when you don't," Angela finished. "Mother is very good at that."

"Yes, and with the babies coming, it's good to know she'll be around. Not having a mother of my own here, I think I'd be lost without yours to rely on."

That spurred a thought Angela hadn't had in a long time. "What about your adoptive mother? Rita? Was that her name? Doesn't she keep in contact anymore?"

"Occasionally we hear something from her, but seldom. We weren't close in my growing up years, and I guess our relationship never will be what it could have been," Micah answered. "I did hear from Dad the other day. He's excited about the babies. He's hoping to be free to come and see them within the next year or so. Things are looking up for him."

"I'm glad," Angela said. "It will be good for him to get to enjoy his grandkids." She looked through the window. "Here they come. I'll introduce you to Adam."

"I can't believe you're marrying someone I've never even met. How did we ever get so far apart?"

"Your husband agreed to pastor that church in southern Ohio, as you will recall. Tell him next time to try to find something closer to home." Angela walked to the back door. "We wouldn't even have you here with us today if he hadn't dropped you off on his way to that conference."

"He was worried about leaving me alone overnight."

"He *should* be at this stage of your pregnancy," Angela said as she pulled open the door. "Hi," she said, and smiled broadly as Heather, Grace and Adam entered the kitchen. "You decided to join us inside for a while?"

"Mom, did you tell Aunt Micah about the wedding?" Heather asked in an out-of-breath voice. "Did you?"

"Yes, she told me," Micah answered and placed an arm around the little girl who had come to her for a hug.

"Where's Grandpa?" Heather asked next.

"He's out back unloading some firewood we had delivered this morning," Grace replied. She reached into the cabinet for cups. "He'll be here soon, I'm sure. He's trying to beat the rain. Coffee, anyone?"

"Yes!" Heather responded.

"No thanks, Mom," Angela said, casting a slight frown in her daughter's direction. "We can't stay. Oh, Micah—this is Adam," Angela said as Adam's arm went easily around her shoulders, pulling her closer. "And Adam—this is Micah, my sister-in-law."

"Rob's wife," he said warmly and stepped forward to shake the hand that Micah extended. "It's nice to meet you."

"You, too, Adam," Micah responded. "And it's wonderful to see Angela so happy. Thanks for your part in that."

He smiled but looked over in time to catch the straight glance Grace had sent his way. Angela's happiness was hanging by a thread, and they both knew it. He had to tell her. Soon. But then he'd known that for too long, hadn't he? This acute sense of regret burning in him now would only be relieved by the truth, but what would that cost him?

"He attends the same church you went to before Rob took you away from everyone," Angela explained.

"Oh, then you might know Carole. She's a friend of mine who attends there now with her husband. Brian Andrews. He is the youth pastor."

"Yes, I've met them. They're a good couple for that ministry. They put a lot of time into it."

"So I hear. They really enjoy the kids," Micah answered.

"Okay, c'mon." Angela spoke to Heather. "Let's go find Grandpa and the boys. Then we've got to go. See you later, Mom. Micah, take care of yourself." She leaned forward to kiss her sister-in-law on the temple. "Why don't you come over tomorrow after Rob gets back from the conference? It would give him a chance to meet Adam."

"That's a great idea. We'll probably do that," Micah answered. "See you then."

Adam felt Grace's silence, but Angela seemed too caught up in the emotion of the day to notice her mother's lack of conversation. Angela gave her mom a brief hug good-bye, and the three of them left the house in search of Ed and the boys. Before long, they were on their way home.

"Will we be moving into your house, Adam? If we do, can we get a dog?" Nathan asked.

Adam glanced in Angela's direction. He had no problem with that idea, but he wasn't certain of her response. And he had to be careful about getting Nathan's hopes up too high—about anything—until he'd talked to Angela privately. "My home isn't very large, but it's bigger than your apartment. It could do for a while." *God, help us to work through this,* he prayed silently. *We're too far into this to let it fall apart now.*

"But what about a dog?" Nathan persisted.

Angela looked at Adam's profile as he stared straight ahead, paying attention to the road. He seemed a little too quiet, and the lines etched at the corners of his eyes seemed more prominent, as though he was worried or angry or...something. "A dog would be okay with me, if it's okay with you." She directed her statement to Adam.

A cheer went up from the kids in the back seat, but Adam barely noticed. He was worried and angry, mostly at himself. And alcohol. And secrets. His. He cleared his throat. "Sure, whatever you think," he responded. *Dear God, what will she think when I tell her?*

"Adam," she asked quietly, "is everything okay?"

"Of course," he lied. What else could he say at this moment, in front of the children? "You guys hungry?" He shifted his focus to the three youngsters in the back of the van. When they indicated that they were, he suggested their favorite hamburger restaurant.

Angela had no personal preference as to where they ate—or if they ate. She wanted to know what was bothering Adam. But she realized she'd have to wait to talk to him privately.

After a quick dinner, Adam dropped Angela and the kids at their home. He gave her a light kiss on the forehead and headed back to the center for a couple of hours. He had work that needed to be done, and he wanted time away from Angela so he could decide how to tell her the truth. Tomorrow. He had to get this over with *tomorrow.* After he met Rob.

"Come in," Angela said as she opened her front door to her brother and sister-in-law. "I'm so glad you could come!"

"Are you kidding?" Micah responded. "Rob wouldn't miss a chance to meet this new man in your life. After all he's heard about him?" She glanced over at Rob to encourage a comment.

"Yes," he halfheartedly agreed. "Micah is right. I'm here to meet Adam. Just as you requested."

Angela took their coats and hung them in the hallway. "He's in the boys' bedroom with them. They are showing him a three-dimensional puzzle of the White House they've been working on all week. Come in. Have a seat. I'm making coffee but it's not ready yet. How did the conference go?"

"Okay, but kind of boring," Rob responded. "I spent most of my time worrying about my wife." He smiled at Micah and leaned close enough to kiss her soft auburn curls.

"Hi, Aunt Micah, Uncle Rob," Heather greeted them after coming around the corner from the hallway. "How are the babies?" She gave her aunt a hug that mostly consisted of embracing Micah's round abdomen.

Micah said, "Hi, sweetie."

"How's my girl?" Rob asked and reached for Heather, scooping her up in his arms. "You've been good?"

"Always," Heather replied, bringing a groan and a sideways glance from her mother. "Mostly," she corrected.

"'Mostly' is fine, if you ask me," Rob replied before he let her go. "And the boys?"

"They're fine," Angela assured them and then whispered, "Even Nathan. He's finally admitted he likes Adam." Angela's news brought a smile to Micah's face.

"I'm so glad," Micah remarked. "I thought he would if you gave him enough time."

"Have a seat, you two. There's no need to stand around in this entryway talking. Micah, could I get you a drink or something? I have a couple of pies in the kitchen if anyone wants a piece."

"No, thank you," Micah said. "I've consumed enough calories for one day. I would take a glass of water, though."

Just as Angela disappeared into the kitchen, Adam and the boys came into the living room from the back hallway.

Rob looked up. "Hello," he said, and walked toward Adam to extend an arm for a handshake. "You must be Adam. Liz has told us a lot about you." Rob glanced over at his very pregnant wife seated somewhat comfortably on the sofa. "I think you've already met my wife."

"And our as-yet-unnamed children," Micah added, patting her belly.

Adam smiled. "It's good to meet you, Rob and, yes, I met Micah yesterday. How are you feeling?" he asked.

"Well enough, I guess," she answered with a friendly smile.

"I'm curious. Why did you use the name 'Liz'?" Adam asked. Angela entered the room at that moment to hand a glass of water to Micah. "I forgot to mention that. My middle name is Elizabeth, and Rob started calling me 'Liz' when I was ten or eleven. I didn't like it—"

"Which is precisely why I did it, if I remember correctly," Rob concluded. He sat down close to Micah and leaned back, resting an arm across the back of the sofa. "She had a way of making things like that a lot of fun."

Angela frowned in Rob's direction. "Anyway, as the years went by, I got used to it. I only have to put up with it from him, so it's not so bad."

"That's your mother's middle name, isn't it?" Micah asked. "And Heather's?"

"Yes," Angela answered, "it is. And Cassie and Carrie's, too. Okay, kids, the pies I made are in the kitchen if you want some. Adam, how about you?"

"No, thank you," he replied. His warm smile matched the look in his eyes as he watched Angela take a seat in the recliner close to Micah. "Pies? When it's not even a holiday?" he teased.

"Sometimes I'll surprise you like that," she answered. "And, if you recall, you recently asked me to marry you, and I'm going to consider that a special occasion."

He studied Angela's face for a moment. She looked contented, buoyant, fully alive. He didn't want to take any of that away from her. She motioned him toward another chair in the small living area. The children all headed for the dessert in the kitchen, leaving the adults to have their conversation in private.

"Nathan, you're in charge of cutting and serving, please," she called to her son. Then she smiled at Adam. She had a good feeling about this. The kids had opened up to him. Certainly Rob could, too. Now if she could just lose that nagging feeling that something wasn't quite right.

Their discussion that day centered on nothing in particular and everything in general. They talked about their spiritual lives and, basically, anything else that came to mind. The conversation flowed easily; and the coffee, freely. At times the kids would pass through—one or two at a time—to add something to their talk, but for the most part it was an "adult" visit.

When Micah yawned, Rob smiled at his sleepy wife. "We should go, hon. You're getting too tired."

"Why don't you rest in my bedroom?" Angela suggested. "You need a nap. You look exhausted." She remembered clearly what the last stages of pregnancy could have to offer: chronic tiredness. At least that's how it had been for Angela all three times. And that was with only one baby. She had trouble imagining what it would be like to be expecting twins.

"If you're sure you don't mind...." Micah agreed and Rob helped her up from the couch. "I'm sorry, guys, but I've gotten used to taking an afternoon nap, and it's a hard habit to break when you're carrying this much weight around."

"I'll walk back with you," Rob said. "She'll need that water." He accepted the glass of water that Angela retrieved from the coffee table. "Thanks. Let's go, Micah."

"Are you okay?" Heather asked when she stuck her head out of her bedroom doorway.

"I'm fine. Just a little tired," Micah responded, and

touched Heather's young face as they passed by on their way to Angela's room.

"Here," Rob said as she eased onto Angela's bed. He set the water on the nightstand and rearranged some pillows the way she liked them. "Are you sure you're just tired? That's all?" He sat down on the edge of the bed and took one of her hands in his. "You've been awfully quiet out there for the last half hour or so."

"I don't know, Rob. I've had a couple of pains...like cramps. But they're gone now." She leaned back into the softness of a pillow.

Rob touched her auburn hair, brushing a strand away from her face. "Maybe we should go home. I'll call the doctor."

"No," she said and squeezed his hand. "Just let me rest for a while. I think I'm okay."

"But Micah, you're not due for—"

"I know,' she answered with a tender smile. "Quit worrying. Go spend some time with your sister and your future brother-in-law. I'm feeling fine now."

"You really think she'll marry him?" Rob asked quietly.

"I'm certain of it. Didn't you notice the way they *are* together? How they look at each other a little longer than necessary? How he squeezed her hand after she handed him the coffee? Even the *way* Angela smiles and how *much* she smiles. She's in love with that man."

"I don't think that means she'll actually marry him," he countered. "I know her pretty well and—"

"You don't know her as well as I do—at least, not at this moment, you don't." Micah's comment obviously surprised Rob and he frowned.

"Honey, she's my sister."

"Yes, and that's the only way you think of her. You know 'Liz'—the eleven-year-old she used to be—better than you know Angela now. You grew up with her, knew her through childhood, her teen years, college...and the beginning of a rocky relationship with Dan. But she's so much more than all of that, Rob. I didn't meet Angela until she was thirty years old, had three kids and was basically the head of her household. She's very intelligent, a wonderful teacher and I'm sure a very capable principal. She's good at handling money, a great parent—look how well she's done with those children and mostly on her own—and she is a strong Christian. Angela and I have prayed together, cried together.... Honey, I know the woman she is today better than you do." Micah paused, letting all that she was saying sink in. "She wants your approval on this, but she doesn't need it. In the end, she'll do what she feels God wants her to do and that will be whatever would be best for her own future and the kids. Don't be hurt or surprised when that decision includes marriage to Adam Dalton."

Rob listened without interruption, which wasn't all that easy for him, and he didn't speak right away after Micah's words had died out. Then his mouth turned up in a half grin. "That's a strong argument you have there, Mrs. Granston. Have you ever considered law school?"

"No," she answered with emphasis. "I want to be a pastor's wife and the mother of twins."

"Lucky you met me, huh?" he teased as he leaned forward to kiss her forehead.

"Luck had nothing to do with it." Micah reached up to gently touch his face. "God arranges these things. Didn't you know that?"

"I know," he agreed, then he pulled away from her and stood up. "What I *don't* know is what I would do without you."

Micah sighed somewhat theatrically. "You'd be wandering aimlessly in a desert somewhere without my love and guidance, no doubt."

Rob laughed quietly. "No doubt."

"Now go—before Angela thinks we've both fallen asleep back here."

"I'll check on you in a few minutes," he said. Then he returned to the living room to get to know Adam Dalton *and* Angela a little better.

"So...what do you think? Of Adam, I mean," Angela asked rather tentatively after Micah had awakened from her nap and rejoined Angela and Rob in the living room. Adam had already left to go to the center for the remainder of the day, and all three children had gone over to the neighbor's house to visit friends.

When Rob didn't reply, Micah did. "I like him, Angela. He's been really good with the kids, and I think he's very kind and caring—very loving toward you.'' She nudged Rob a little from where she sat next to him on the couch.

Rob frowned, not an unusual reaction to Angela's choice of men in her life. ''Micah and I don't entirely agree on this. Think about it. What do you really know about this guy? You've only been out with him a few times—''

''We've been dating for nearly two months, Rob,'' Angela corrected. ''I know that's not long, but he's different from Dan if that's what you're worried about.''

''The only thing I'm worried about is you. Your first marriage was a disaster, almost from beginning to end. I don't want to see another mistake in your life.''

''And you think I do?'' she replied with a sigh. ''I don't even know if I could survive another mistake, Rob. No one is more afraid of that than me.''

''Then don't rush into this thing,'' he advised bluntly.

''Maybe I'll go to the kitchen and make some more coffee. Rob, help me up, please,'' Micah said quickly, looking down at the pastel swirls of her very full maternity top. Rob stood to pull her to her feet. ''It's been a while,'' she commented, ''since I've been able to get off a couch without help.''

''No, Micah, stay, please,'' Angela protested.

''This argument is between a brother and a sister. I don't feel right being included.''

Rob let go of Micah's hand and leaned forward to

kiss the top of her head. "Stay, hon. We may need a referee before this is over. You know how stubborn Liz can be."

"Me?" Angela exclaimed. "You're the one who feels so guilty about my first marriage that you refuse to even consider the thought of a second."

"That's not true," he said sharply, but when Angela raised her eyebrows in obvious disagreement, he relented. "All right, maybe it is true. You shouldn't have married Dan, you shouldn't have ever dated him, and I should have been there."

"To do what? Rescue me? You're not my keeper, Robert. I'm not your responsibility. I never was."

"I know that, but still—"

"What good do you think you could have done me? Recalling some of your dumb stunts, you were barely able to watch out for yourself in those days."

"Don't remind me," he responded as he sat down again next to Micah. Rob leaned forward slightly, rubbing his forehead with his right hand. Micah touched her husband's shoulder. She knew better than anyone how deeply this issue bothered him. She'd been there when it kept sleep away.

"Rob, the point is, I don't *blame* you. It was my own stupid fault. No one else's. Not even Dan's. I could have told him to get lost from the very beginning. *I* am the one who made bad decisions. I shouldn't have dated him, shouldn't have slept with him, shouldn't have gotten pregnant. They are *my* mistakes—*mine.* You can't claim them. I won't let you." Angela knelt on the floor in front of her brother, whose face was now buried in his hands. She reached for his arm, but he didn't look up. "Let yourself off the hook for this, Rob. You preach to others about forgiveness. Why don't you practice a little of it for yourself?"

He shook his head. "Liz, all those years...Dan's drinking, your divorce...." he began, but his words died out in the comfort of his sister's embrace.

Micah's eyes flooded with tears. Rob had carried that guilt far too long, and Angela's words had provided his release. Micah heard her husband's broken words. "I'm so sorry."

"Don't be," Angela offered through tears of her own. "I'm not. Not anymore. Think of the kids, Rob. I wouldn't have any of them if I hadn't had Dan in my life. I'd go through all of it again to have them."

"I know." He nodded. "I know. God has a way of bringing something good out of all of it." He hugged Angela tightly, then pulled a handkerchief from his pocket to wipe his eyes. Micah grabbed a few tissues from the box on the coffee table and shared them with Angela.

Angela laughed softly. "Well, this is a fine scene. Three adults crying all over each other." When their laughter blended together, she reached over to hug Micah warmly.

"Just don't tell Adam this is what happened when you asked us what we thought of him," Micah suggested. "He might misunderstand."

"True," Angela responded. "But you know, in all

seriousness, Adam is wonderful. Once you get to know him better, you'll love him."

"And you already do," Micah remarked. She had suddenly noticed a light in her sister-in-law's eyes that she'd not seen there before.

Angela nodded. "Very much. And he's been a Christian for seven years. He's really serious about it, Rob."

Rob smiled. "Don't worry. I'll be nice to him."

"What I want is for you to be a *brother* to him." Angela went on, "I want this man in my life until 'death do us part.' And I want *you* to be the minister to marry us—and do it with happiness. You got that?" She gave the command with a playful punch to his arm.

"Yes." He laughed. "I'll follow orders."

"If you'll open your heart to the possibilities, you won't need orders. You'll love him, too," Angela added, then became suddenly quiet. "Adam is the only man in this world I've ever loved more than you." Angela had spoken her heart and she touched Rob's cheek gently. "And if either of you two tell Dad or Eric I said that, you're in big trouble."

Rob smiled just as Micah broke down in tears. He and Angela both turned to her immediately. "Honey, are you okay?" Rob asked. "What's wrong?"

"Nothing. It's just so sweet to see you and Angela working this out after all these years. It makes me....so happy...." she said on the edge of a sob. Then she virtually melted into Rob's embrace, burying her face in his shoulder.

Angela grinned and shook her head. "I think she's still in her everything-makes-me-cry mode."

"I'm sorry…I can't help it…." Micah managed to say the muffled words in between sobs. "Maybe we'll have a boy and a girl, brother and sister. And maybe they'll be close…just like you are…."

Rob kissed her cheek gently. "It's okay, hon. Cry if you want to."

"I'll leave you two alone," Angela said. She stood up, raising her hand to prevent Rob from standing and disturbing Micah's comfortable position against him. "Don't get up. Let her cry. She'll feel better afterwards. I'm going to shower and change, so you can let yourselves out when you're ready to leave. I'll call you later about the wedding." She left them alone, heading back down the hallway to the bathroom. She remembered her own crying jags during three pregnancies and wondered briefly how long it would take for Micah to be done with the tears tonight. Not that it mattered. However long it lasted, Rob would be there. Just as she knew Adam would be.

Adam dialed Angela's number with deliberation. He'd put this off long enough.

"Hello." She answered the phone on the first ring.

"Hi, I'm finished up here for the night, and it's still early. Are Rob and Micah still there?"

"No, they left a little while ago."

"Want to take the kids out for a pizza?" he asked. Afterwards, he would talk to her—openly, honestly—as he knew he should have done from the beginning.

"Yes," she replied. "Are you coming over now?"

"In about twenty minutes. And Angela, after dinner...we need to talk about something. Just the two of us."

"All right," she agreed. "We will." She'd be relieved to find out what had been bothering him for the past few days.

Within an hour, they had found seats in their favorite pizza parlor. They were ordering their dinner when they were greeted at the table by some people unfamiliar to Angela: Allen and Bonita Dalton, Adam's brother and sister-in-law. And Tiffany was with them. Adam, Angela sensed, was not overly pleased with this encounter, but polite introductions were made. Bonita was Tiffany's mother, and they looked enough alike to confirm it.

"You're the woman Tiffany mentioned when we were looking at wedding gowns. Isn't she, sweetheart?" Bonita asked her daughter, and Tiffany agreed.

"Yes, I remarked on how much I like your taste in clothing. You always look so elegant and well put together, no matter what the occasion is."

Angela's mouth nearly dropped open in surprise, but she caught herself and carefully guarded her response for fear of hurting the girl's feelings. Hadn't this been the gorgeous young woman who had looked so incredibly...female in that skirt and sweater on the night of the Open House? She certainly wasn't someone Angela expected to be seeking her advice on fashion. "Thank you. That's quite a compliment."

“Perhaps Angela would be willing to go shopping with you to find the kind of dress you’re looking for. After all, she’ll be part of the family soon, and you haven’t liked anything I’ve suggested so far,” Bonita suggested. Angela agreed to do so if that was really what Tiffany wanted. The tentative date was set for the first Saturday afternoon that they both had free. Then Tiffany left the restaurant to meet her fiancé for a late date, leaving Allen and Bonita to join Adam, Angela and the kids for a meal. The pizza tasted hot and spicy and the kids drank far too much soda pop to please Angela. The conversation went well, with talk of Adam and Angela’s future, as well as Tiffany’s wedding plans. When the discussion among the adults lagged, the kids picked it up again by asking questions about Bonita’s work as a veterinarian’s assistant. In fact, she had a homeless mother cat and kittens sitting in pet carriers in her car at that moment. She was taking them home for a few days, in hopes of finding a new owner. Angela let the kids go outside with Bonita to see the animals—on the understanding that under no circumstance were they taking one home. Not if a new puppy was a possibility in the near future. So Angela and Allen were left sitting at the table while Adam walked up to the register to pay for their dinner.

Adam didn’t like leaving her alone with his brother, but he decided against making an issue of it. He’d only be away for a minute or two to take care of the check. How much damage could be done in a few minutes? But the cashier was slower than Adam would have liked. By the time he made his way back to their table, Angela was nowhere to be seen, and Allen had a rather guilty look about him that Adam had seen before.

"Where's Angela?" he asked, returning his wallet to his back pocket as he spoke.

"She went outside to the van. She seemed kind of upset about something, Adam. You'd better go."

"What upset her?" he asked, his heart sinking. He thought he knew the answer.

"I don't know. We were just joking around about college days and—"

Adam swallowed hard, trying not to let his anger show. But his curt voice conveyed his feelings well enough. "You had to bring that up, I suppose. About the weekends and all? Allen, I would think you could handle a five-minute conversation with her without talking about it."

"Well, yeah, but—"

"I want to marry this woman," Adam stated, his eyes lit with anger. "Do you really think she wanted to hear about that from you? Or do you just enjoy telling it?"

"Adam—"

"Clean up your own life, Allen, and stop being jealous that I've already taken care of mine." With those harsh words he walked out of the restaurant. He saw her, standing by the van in the chilly night air.

"Angela... Angie!" he called to her. But at the sound of her name, she turned her back to him and leaned against the vehicle. As he came up behind her, he realized her shoulders were shaking from crying. His heart broke for her—from the pain he'd inflicted.

"Angie, we need to talk."

"It's a little late for that," she replied in a choking voice. She took a deep breath. She needed to calm down, to walk around to the other side of the van and get in. The kids were across the street in the lot looking at Bonita's kittens, and she had to get them into the van and leave without having this argument with Adam right here in front of them. All she wanted now was to go home and have a good cry—and then start trying to forget Adam Dalton. Liar that he was.

Then he was near her, touching her shoulder.

"Leave me alone," she stated, moving away from him. She turned and looked him right in the eyes, wanting to hurt him as badly as he had hurt her. "You've lied to me all along, haven't you? And I thought we had something special...."

"We do, Angie. I did not lie to you," he insisted. He reached for her arm to stop her from running away. "I just hadn't told you yet."

"Tell me, Adam, when do you think you might have gotten around to letting me know? On the honeymoon?"

He gripped her arm, halting her in her tracks. "I would have told you soon—when the time was right."

"Just when is a 'right time' to tell someone you're an alcoholic? Maybe you should consider mentioning it right up front. Especially to a woman whose first husband nearly wrecked her life with the same problem!'' She attempted to shrug off his grip on her but was no match for him as he held her almost effortlessly.

"I should have told you in the park as soon as I found out about Dan. You'd never mentioned he was an alcoholic. Why didn't you say so earlier? Angela, I'd already said that I wanted you *forever*—that was before you told me about the drinking. What was I supposed to do? Tell you, then and there? Risk losing you—"

"Yes! Why didn't you?" she demanded.

"Because I knew how you'd react. Just like this—angry, frightened, hopeless. And I knew you'd run away."

"Can you blame me? I've spent the last dozen years of my life dealing with alcoholism and its horrendous effects on my family, my kids! Do you think I'd willingly sign on for more of the same?" Tears burned a path down her cheeks, and she looked away, wiping them with her fingers. If she could just get her children into the van and drive away from here, away from him...so she could be angry and sad and miserable. Alone.

"I don't blame you for being upset, but this is a problem we can live with. It's nothing like what you've been through with Dan."

"You don't know what I've been through with him. And you don't know how it will be with you. Do all drinkers have the mistaken idea that their problem is 'under control'? What is it with you guys, anyway? Would it threaten your manly pride to admit that you're *not* in control? That you need help? From God, from counselors, from someone!"

"When I needed help, I found it. We'll be okay with this, Angie. I know we will. I still go to the weekly meetings—"

"And what? Weekly meetings are going to save our marriage? I don't think so, Adam. I'm sure you're trying and things are going well now, but I can't take a risk like that. I can't have both you and sanity in my life—and I choose sanity."

Adam stood silently staring at her, understanding her fears but wanting her to overcome them enough to give them this chance. "We'll be okay with this, Angie. I love you too much to risk hurting you or the kids," he responded. "I need you to trust me."

"Trust you?! How can I do that when you don't tell me the truth?" she cried, anguish searing her heart. "Adam, how could you let me think this could work? That I could have a second chance? That I could have *you?*" She turned from him in complete despair as he released her arm. Deep sobs racked her body, and Adam placed a hand gently on her back, wanting to comfort her, and yet knowing that he was the source of the pain. When Angela had taken several deep breaths and regained a fragile control over her emotions, she faced him again—to lash out at him, to tell him goodbye forever. But the bleak sorrow she saw in his expression startled her and momentarily silenced her.

Adam sighed heavily, and with a voice weighed with regret he spoke first. "I would have told you,

Angela. It's not a secret I wanted to keep. But I needed time with you to prove that I could be trusted with other things—smaller things—before I had to ask you to trust me with this."

She shook her head, unable to speak without emotion. She *couldn't* trust him. Not with this. And cold despair settled over her at the thought of a future—dark and lonely—without him.

"You've been a Christian a long time, you know," Adam offered in a still voice. He shoved his cold hands deep into his pockets. "Since when has alcoholism become something that can't be forgiven?"

"I could forgive you for just about anything," she replied softly. Then she reached up, touching his cheek with tenderness. "But I won't live with this."

Adam's expression remained grim as he watched her walk away. And Angela didn't look back while opening the van door for her approaching children.

"Hey, Adam, aren't you coming with us?" Nathan called out before he was ushered into the vehicle by his impatient mother.

"He's going to ride home with Allen and Bonita," Angela explained in a voice that sounded far more under control than she felt. "I need to talk to you guys alone for a few minutes." She glanced up once through watery eyes to see Adam watching them from where he stood on the sidewalk in the shadows of nightfall. She missed him deeply—even now, when she knew the real loneliness hadn't yet begun. Swallowing a sob that rose in her throat, she tried to think clearly; she had to say something appropriate to the children. She didn't want them hating her for putting an end to their hopes. And she didn't want them to hate Adam...for anything. She knew *she* never would.

The call came in the middle of the night. It was one of those calls no one likes to get. Grace let Angela know that Rob had taken Micah to the hospital. Micah was in premature labor that couldn't be stopped, so the babies were coming. Six weeks early. Grace said what Angela already knew—that the only thing to be done at this point was to pray. So while Grace and Ed headed toward the hospital, Angela prayed.

As morning came and Angela and the children went through their daily routine, Angela's thoughts were never far from Micah. The day seemed to drag by, but finally they returned home from school. Angela called her parents' home, but the answering machine came on. No one was home yet. She called Eric and Hope, but there was no answer there, either. So she turned the oven on and reached for a box of frozen fish sticks and a bag of French fries so she could get supper started. Then came the phone call from Rob that she'd been waiting for.

"Liz?"

"Rob?" Angela dropped the food she was holding on the counter. "Is Micah all right? What happened?"

"She's okay, thank the Lord. Exhausted, but all right. She's sleeping now. The babies...oh, Liz, you ought to see them. They're amazing. Beautiful. Small, but not like we thought. Five pounds, two ounces and five pounds, four ounces. Nicholas is bigger—"

"Rob, that's lovely! Naming your son after Nicky."

"Nicholas—" Rob cleared his throat as his voice broke with emotion "—Nicholas Edward and Natalie Elizabeth."

Angela's eyes flooded with tears. "Same middle name as most of the Granston females, huh?"

"Well, you know how it is once a precedent has been set."

"Thank God they're all safe and sound," Angela said softly.

"He's so good to us, Liz. Sometimes I don't have the words."

"I know. *He* knows." She paused. "Give Micah a kiss for me. The kids and I will drive down after school tomorrow to see your new family. Do they have evening visiting hours?"

"Yes, and you've got to come. They're absolutely gorgeous. Perfect. You've got to see them. And Micah—" He hesitated. "I felt so badly for her last night, Liz. No parents to call...and she was scared. When Mom and Dad showed up, it meant the world to her."

"I'm sure it did. I'm so sorry I couldn't have been there, too."

"That's okay. You shouldn't bring your kids out in the middle of the night to sit in a hospital waiting room for hours. But come when you can, and bring

Adam. My guess is you'll be the next member of the family in labor and delivery."

Angela's tears increased from a trickle to a steady flow, but she didn't try to explain why Adam wouldn't be with her. She just told her brother she'd see him soon, and hung up. The next baby in the family belonging to Angela and Adam? It had been a beautiful idea that had vanished along with the marriage plans. Yesterday another child had seemed possible. Today another wedding in the family seemed out of the question.

Chapter Twelve

Angela flipped open the Sunday School booklet in her hand. Once again, she had been too busy this week to study the lesson, and she noticed they were nearing the end of the book signaling the completion of the fall quarter. Thanksgiving was less than two weeks away, and her engagement to Adam ended over two weeks ago. Time flies, apparently whether you're having fun or not, Angela concluded.

She quickly looked over the lesson for today. Lately, reviewing the weekly Sunday School material wasn't anywhere near the top of her list of "things to do." Neither were her usual morning devotions or prayer time—not that she was sleeping later or purposefully avoiding those responsibilities. They were just easy to let slip by. She had no one to be accountable to. No one except the Lord, of course, and she hadn't felt particularly close to Him lately, either.

The one bright spot in the string of days that

seemed to all run together had been a pleasant surprise: shopping with Tiffany yesterday. She'd been uncertain about going through with the plan in the aftermath of her breakup with Adam, but Tiffany had called her to ask if she would help her pick out an outfit for the upcoming awards ceremony at the center. The wedding dress could wait, but Tiffany needed something appropriate for the awards night. She wasn't sure exactly what Adam needed her to help with that night, but she knew she'd at least be handing out certificates, and she wanted to look appropriate in front of the many parents and friends of the center.

"If you're sure you want my help, I'll be glad to go," Angela had agreed with a little hesitancy. She couldn't imagine how the shopping trip would go, but she was willing to give it a try. Much to her surprise, it proved to be fun. And interesting.

"I still haven't found the right wedding gown," the young woman had lamented as they looked through racks of clothes at Angela's favorite dress shop in the mall near her home. She loved the clothes, and even more than that she loved the short drive to a facility filled with so many great stores all under one roof—one now very heavily decorated for Christmas.

"Don't worry, you'll find something you like soon," Angela assured her. "Have you considered a less traditional dress? Maybe one of those Victorian clothing catalogs?"

"That's a great idea. I love that style of clothing," Tiffany exclaimed, pushing some dark strands of hair from her forehead. Picking up a bright pink jacket, she held it up for Angela to consider.

"I think a softer color would be better, more formal. What do you think of this shade of red?" Angela held up a suit for Tiffany's inspection and received a smile in response.

"Let me try it on," Tiffany said, taking the hanger from Angela and heading toward the dressing room. "Would this white blouse be good with it?" she asked, pulling an elegant-looking sheer white blouse from the display outside the dressing room door.

"Umm." Angela stalled for a moment as she glanced through the clothing. "Possibly. But let's try a couple of these, too. This one with the small red print might look nice." She handed a few choices to Tiffany, who took them gratefully before disappearing down a narrow hallway to change.

Within minutes, the young woman had put on the outfit and was modeling it for Angela in front of a three-way mirror. "I like it," Tiffany said as she turned around to view her back in the reflection. "What do you think? Is it too loose?"

"No," Angela replied quickly. "I think it's just right. Very professional-looking for a professional young woman. That's what you are, you know."

"I really enjoy working at the center. I'd like to be thought of as someone capable of running a facility like that by myself someday soon." The downcast expression on Tiffany's face took Angela by surprise. "Unless I change my image, I'll never reach my goals. I need to be able to support myself for the day

I'm on my own. Just like you. You know, there's a good chance this marriage to Cameron won't last."

Angela stood looking at Tiffany, considering her words and her youth. "If you're uncertain about this marriage, why don't you and Cameron wait for a while? You don't need to rush into anything. You're so young."

"That's what everyone says, but I don't *feel* young. You know? I mean, I feel like it's time to be married, to settle down...to change." She took another look at the suit, just as Angela took another look at Tiffany, who was not the college kid she sometimes appeared to be. "I guess I should take this off. I like it, though. Do you?"

Angela smiled. "Definitely. It looks great on you."

Tiffany was only gone for a few minutes and then reappeared in the jeans and sweatshirt she'd worn into the store. "I'll take these," she told the salesclerk and pulled a credit card from her back pocket.

After the purchase was made, they left the store and walked down the mallway, finding an appropriate pair of shoes and even a pair of earrings to go with Tiffany's outfit before they finished shopping.

"Do you go to church, Tiffany?" Angela asked as they walked toward the exit.

"No," she answered. "Not that Adam hasn't invited us plenty of times. We've just not taken him up on it."

"Your mother and Allen don't go?"

"Neither one of them went to church when they were growing up, and of course I didn't, either. I think that plays a large part in how much interest you have in religion as an adult. At least, I always did think that until I met Adam. I guess he kind of proves that theory wrong, doesn't he? Growing up in the same house with Allen, yet turning out so differently."

Angela's smile was bittersweet as she thought of Adam. He was a changed man. God had taken care of that. Didn't she trust God to continue to take care of that?

"There really must be something to this idea of help from a higher power, you know?" Tiffany added. "There has to be. How else could Adam be so changed and Allen remain so much the same? Allen's tried to give up drinking a million times, and it never lasts. Not for long, that is."

"You can have a personal relationship with the Lord, just like Adam and I have. He doesn't have to be thought of as some distant source of higher power. He's real. He can be with you, helping you daily. I wouldn't want to see what my life would be without Him, and I'm certain Adam would say the same."

"He'd have to." Tiffany agreed wholeheartedly. "To keep from drinking now, when he's lost you? Something must be holding him together."

They pushed open the exit doors and stepped out into a cold November chill. It was a long walk to the van, and all the way there, Angela thought of Adam. What if he didn't take a drink now, at this time in his life? Was it proof enough for her? Was it enough evidence to convince her that alcohol would never again have an impact on her life? Or her children's?

And where was her answer from God? She was beginning to feel like the woman in Luke 18 who kept going to a judge with the same pleas until finally he granted her wish so she would quit bothering him with the request. Eventually, one way or another, the Lord had to let Angela know which road to follow. He *had* to. It wasn't a decision she could make on her own.

"Adam is a good man, Angela," Tiffany said once they were inside the vehicle with the engine running. "I hope you know that about him."

"I do," she answered quickly, truthfully. "There's nothing easy about walking away from him. But with kids—"

"I know. I grew up with Allen's drinking, and it wasn't easy. I didn't invite friends over much, didn't count on him for help with anything—homework, boy trouble, anything. It was difficult. But with Adam...." She paused. "I just can't see him slipping back into that old life, you know? He's different from Allen—inside and out. Sometimes I'm kind of envious of him really. I know he's working too hard right now—too many hours, too many projects—to keep his mind off you, I suppose. But still, he has a calmness about him—confidence, assurance...peace, I guess you could say. I'd like to feel that way, too."

"You could, Tiffany. Come to church with me sometime. Or come over to my home, and I'll show you some things the Bible has to say about the peace of God. It can be as real for you as it is for Adam or for me."

"I suppose," she replied with a smile. "Maybe I will. Thanks for the offer. And thanks for helping me with my shopping. I really like the outfit." When Angela said goodbye to Tiffany later that day, it was with a genuine fondness.

She was thinking of some of the young woman's comments when she realized that the Scripture lesson of the morning was being read by the pastor's wife, who happened to be sitting next to Angela in the Sunday School class. She tried to block out the many other thoughts that occupied her mind to listen—really listen—to God's word. That was something she hadn't done much of these past few weeks and, even now, her concentration was diverted to thoughts of Adam.

He had deceived her. True, it was something he had *not* told her rather than anything he'd actually done. But it was deceit all the same. He knew what she'd been through with Dan, and yet he let her think life would be different with him. Sure, it would be different in the beginning, but he *was* an alcoholic. Recovering, yes, but he'd always be an alcoholic. Salvation hadn't changed that. The temptation to drink would always be there, regardless of what God had done in his heart. He couldn't be the man for her. The Lord wouldn't expect her to take such a risk, to trust *that* much. And if he did expect that much of her, He would have to make it clear to her. Plain and simple.

The pastor's wife read on and soon she was telling of Peter's visions of the great sheet with four corners being let down to the earth with all manner of beasts in it. She read how the voice of God told Peter to kill and eat, and how Peter refused to eat anything that was ceremonially unclean. He was still living by the Mosaic system despite living in the age of grace. "Do not call anything impure that God had made clean." Acts 10:15b made it clear that Peter could eat anything because God had said so. That was reason enough. God had said so. Angela knew the story frontward and backward, and impatiently wondered what new light the teacher could shed on this subject of the acceptance of Gentiles by God. Certainly these verses could be symbolic of many things, especially people. When people are saved, they are changed, their lives are changed. Don't doubt God on it. Trust Him. Accept them. Angela sat up a little straighter and reached for the cup of coffee she'd left beside her chair. Just then the teacher rephrased a thought: "What God finds acceptable, don't you call unacceptable." As she spoke, she looked directly at Angela. Angela nearly dropped her foam cup.

God had accepted Adam. It was just that simple. How could she think of him as unacceptable? "Are we to set our standards higher than the Lord's?" the teacher asked. The discussion turned toward the fact that Gentiles, too, had been given the privilege of turning to Christ and receiving forgiveness for their sins and eternal life, but Angela heard little else as the morning progressed. Her mind kept wandering back to Adam. She tried to understand his reasons for not telling her the truth in the very beginning. Maybe it simply had been as he said. He needed her to trust him with smaller things before he could ask her to trust him over the alcoholism. There had been no real reason to think Adam had known about Dan's drinking problems back when Adam began seeing her. She hadn't told him. Maybe no one else had, either.

"Angela? Are you all right?" She looked up at the mention of her name. The classroom was nearly empty, and her Sunday School teacher was rather noisily returning some reference books to the shelf while studying Angela's frowning face. "The dismissal bell rang several minutes ago."

"Oh," Angela said, and quickly gathered up her Bible, lesson book and purse. "...I guess I let my mind wander. Sorry." She tossed her empty coffee cup into the trash can and smiled. "See you downstairs in the sanctuary."

"All right. See you then," the teacher responded.

Angela made her exit quickly and paused at the water fountain in the hallway. "What God finds acceptable, don't you call unacceptable." The emphatic statement certainly seemed meant for her. But how could she know—absolutely, positively know—she could accept Adam into her life? Forever. *And it isn't just* my *future in question here, Lord. There are three kids involved, too. Remember?* she thought silently as the cool water flowed across her dry lips. She would need some confirmation. Loving Adam as deeply as she did, she would not go to him until she felt certain that it was the Lord's will. "That's the only way we'll be able to make it work. The only way," she whispered to herself.

And if the Lord was going to give her the answer she needed, she hoped he would give it soon. Tomorrow night was the annual awards ceremony at the recreation center. Angela and the children would be there; most likely, so would the director. Now if she could just figure out a way to leave her heart at home....

When Angela and her children entered the recreation center, a brisk gust of wind blew in behind them. It was a cold November, and the continuous threat of snow in the forecast had caused Heather to suggest that Thanksgiving might seem more like Christmas this year. But whether it snowed or not, this promised to be a cold holiday for Angela. Maybe all the rest of them would be, too.

A young usher wearing a bright red blazer handed Angela a program and smiled. Angela smiled back and wondered if Tiffany would be wearing the suit they had selected. It had looked lovely on her—perfect for this annual awards ceremony. Though even Tiffany hadn't been sure how large a part she'd play in tonight's festivities. This event had always fallen mostly to the director.

"I don't see Adam," Heather commented, craning her neck to peer around her brothers. "He's got to be here somewhere."

Angela knew Heather was right. This was his domain. He had to be here...somewhere. *And Lord, don't let it be near me*, Angela prayed silently.

They walked toward the auditorium, worked their

way through the crowd of spectators, and found a place to sit.

"This is perfect, Mom." Heather climbed up into the bleachers. "You can see me fine from here." Angela smiled and agreed. Heather was to be on the platform tonight to receive an award for swimming class—"Most Improved"—along with her certificate of completion. She'd overcome her fears and made the mandatory dive on the last night of class. With some encouragement, of course, from someone she trusted. Angela glanced around the room, looking for that someone. She did owe him a thank-you for his help. Her six-year-old daughter had trusted him. Why couldn't she? And were those her thoughts, or was the Lord trying to get through to her? How would she ever know?

"Mom, could we go get some snacks? Popcorn or something? I have money with me," Nathan added. Angela followed his line of vision to a concession booth on the other side of the auditorium.

"Sure, you can go," she replied, watching David and Heather scramble after their older brother. "Guys, keep an eye on your sister." She glanced over the program in her hands, looking for Adam's name. But Tiffany was the only staff member listed in charge tonight. It was then that she heard her name spoken from somewhere behind her on the bleachers.

"Adam?" She turned to see him, but he looked different from what she expected. He was casually dressed, tan corduroys and a soft camel-colored shirt.

At least, she thought as she cleared her throat nervously, it *looked* soft. "How are you?"

He shrugged. "All right, I guess. How about you?"

"I'm fine," she answered. She watched him take a seat, uninvited, right where Heather had been sitting only seconds ago. So he *was* here. She had known he would be. "No jacket? No tie?" she commented.

"Nope, it's Tiffany's program tonight. I'm sitting this one out."

"She didn't know that a couple of days ago when I went shopping with her."

"Well, she knows now," he answered offhandedly and nodded toward his raven-haired niece. "She looks good. Very professional. Reserved. I take it you had something to do with that." He tilted his head to look at Angela, the straight line of his mouth and steady gaze showing no hint of the emotion that gnawed at him. He knew this would be it. They'd find some way to work through this mess. They had to. Tonight. If not, then tomorrow he started looking for another job, in another city—somewhere away from all this happiness that he couldn't quite reach.

"She asked for my help," Angela responded. "It seemed like something I should do."

"And you usually do the things you should," he added, then looked away. "So do I."

She closed her eyes momentarily in frustration. "Adam, why are you here…with us? You didn't even need to come to this ceremony."

"Yes, I did," he answered emphatically. "It's called 'keeping a promise.'" He looked back into her eyes and somehow managed to remain expressionless. "I see Heather coming this way, but where are the boys?"

"They all went to get some popcorn and drinks. They'll be back in a moment. I'm sure they'll be surprised to see you."

"Why?" he asked. "I told them I'd be here."

"They're not all that used to a man keeping his word," she answered quietly.

"And neither are you," he said, just as the kids approached them. He was right and they both knew it. The promise had been to Angela, too. As much as was within his power, he'd not let her sit alone through another of the children's programs as she had done for years. But tonight she would have preferred sitting alone to being so close to the man who was breaking her heart.

"Adam!" Heather was the only one of the trio that called out his name, but it was clear to Angela, and to anyone else looking, that the expressions on all three young faces were ones of pleasant surprise.

"How have you been?" David asked, while Heather's greeting was a king-size embrace and a giggle.

"We've missed you," Nathan said. Angela was stunned. Nathan, being the eldest, usually tried to maintain an air of maturity that his siblings obviously lacked. But not tonight. At least, not for long. He watched David offer a big hug, too, and when it was Nathan's turn, Angela saw him start to extend a hand for a handshake. But Adam smiled and shook his head as he reached for the boy. They hugged, with Nathan holding tighter than either of the other two. Angela blinked back tears and looked away.

"I didn't think you'd sit with us," Nathan said in an uneven tone. He cleared his throat rather roughly. "I mean, after you and Mom...." His words died out.

Angela winced. She hadn't meant to hurt the kids by leaving Adam. She'd been trying to protect them. But now, she wondered, from what? Kept promises? A warm embrace?

Adam glanced at Angela, who refused to look up at him. "Your mother and I may not be getting married, but we're not enemies." He tickled Heather in the ribs when she crowded back into his arms. "We can still all sit together without it causing a problem. Can't we, Angie?"

She didn't dare to speak. She couldn't be sure what words would come out. No one called her Angie except Adam—and then usually in tender moments. She nodded her head, still refusing to meet Adam's eyes.

"Mom, you okay?" David asked, studying his mother's downcast profile.

"Yes, hon, I'm okay," she replied. But she wasn't okay, and she didn't think she ever would be again if she couldn't share her life with this man. Why, of all things, was he an alcoholic? She could have dealt with anything else. Then she thought of Patty in the bathrobe. Well, maybe not *anything* else. Adam could have relived old times with Patty and even have created some *new* ones if he had chosen to, perhaps even with a drink or two. It would have been easy enough for him to return to old habits, especially when "old habits" looked as good as his ex-wife. But he had chosen not to, she reminded herself. He'd chosen not to.

Adam's voice jarred her back into the present. "Heather, there's the rest of your swimming class." He pointed across the room to a group of kids. "You need to join them for the awards."

Angela looked over at Adam, watching him direct her daughter. He could be the man to help her direct all of her kids to where they needed to be in life. But not until she overcame her own fears and doubts. Adam seemed to have truly changed from the lifestyle his brother had described to her. But could people really change completely? Be someone different from who they'd been? Dan certainly never could.

"Have you ever thought about how your brother, Rob, has changed over the years?" Adam asked suddenly, his question seeming to come out of the blue. But it wasn't really. He simply knew the conflict raging inside her. It was always the same where he was concerned. Could he change? Could he be trusted? Adam wanted to turn her focus back to the Lord, the source of all their strengths.

Angela looked down again. Could he somehow read her mind? The boys had taken seats on either side of Adam, which left her off to the side with Nathan seated between them. She coughed nervously. "Of course I've thought of that." She had, hadn't she? Rob had completely changed when he was away from the Lord, and then changed again upon returning to his faith. And Micah had a lot to do with it. "The babies were born last week."

"I know. Rob called me."

She turned to him questioningly, but now he was watching the children line up for the presentation. "He called you? Just to tell you that?"

"That, and to give me some advice about you."

"And that advice was...." She was hoping he'd fill in the blank.

"Personal," he replied. "He said the babies are doing fine. Nicholas and Natalie. Good names." He paused. "He asked when I thought we might have one."

"You'd have to get married first," Nathan commented from his position between them. Then he took a bite of the popcorn he and David had been sharing.

The adults glanced at him, then looked at each other, sharing a smile. "I didn't think you were paying any attention to us," Angela said.

"Well, you were wrong," Nathan replied. "Kids are always listening to what grown-ups say." He stood up. "I'm going to move down here with David so you guys can talk about stuff by yourselves."

Angela laughed quietly as Nathan moved beside his younger brother. Suddenly there was a space between Angela and Adam that no one seemed prepared to span. "Rob's case is different from ours."

"You mean 'mine.'" Adam countered. "Because he was called into the ministry, or because he's your hero?"

Anger warmed her cheeks as she said bluntly, "He's not my 'hero.'"

"Yes, he is, and that's okay. He's your brother and you love him. But he's just a man. If he can change, so can I. He even needed the help of Micah to push him in the direction of change. My change came years ago from the hand of the Lord as an answer to prayer. It doesn't hinge on you, or on how well things are going with us. When you walked away from me, it didn't drive me back to—"

"Adam, please, this isn't exactly a private place."

He paused. She was right. This wasn't the place to tell her how much he'd wanted a drink that night. Or how one would have been too much and, at the same time, never enough. "After Heather gets her award, we'll go into my office."

The ceremony began under Tiffany's direction, and when Heather's turn came, she walked up and accepted her certificate of completion and participation ribbon quite proudly. Tiffany commented on how Heather's dive on her final day of class enabled her to pass to the next level. Tiffany held the microphone to Heather, allowing her to speak to the audience.

"Thank you, Adam, for helping me dive," she said simply as she waved to Adam and Angela from the platform. The visitors burst into applause, making Heather the star of the evening.

The program was brief and well done, and Tiffany looked relieved when it concluded.

"Heather told me you walked out on the board with her. It made all the difference in the world to her.'' Angela had heard Heather's account of last week's dive.

Adam and the boys were laughing about something, but he leaned near Angela to respond.

''It surprised me. I thought she'd want me in the water to catch her, but she didn't. It was the walking out on that board all alone that frightened her. The first time I held her arms and lowered her down into the water. The next time, she jumped. By herself.''

Angela shook her head in amazement. Maybe her children's instincts were better than her own. Anything was possible.

''Let's go,'' Adam said, directing her with a firm hand pressed to her back. ''To my office.''

''Nathan, we're going to Adam's office for a few minutes. You may visit with your friends for a while and have some of the refreshments, but keep David and Heather with you. If you need me, you know where to find me.''

Angela followed Adam through the crowd of spectators toward the hallway that led to privacy. Adam switched on the light in the darkened room and closed the door behind him as they entered. Angela's mind returned briefly to the discussion they'd shared the day he asked her to marry him—in the middle of the afternoon at a public park. That day had been so full of happiness and promise. This conversation would be different. Painful, final.

Adam didn't say anything as he approached his desk, taking a seat on the edge. He motioned Angela toward a nearby leather chair.

"Thank you, but I'd rather stand," she replied. She raised her eyes to glance at the clock on the paneled wall, although she really had no concern about the time. It was just someplace to look, other than into the depth of his eyes. Her gaze fell upon a photograph lying on the cabinet not far from where she stood: a snapshot of a dog. Nathan's dog. "Adam, where did you get that picture of Max? I don't remember taking it." She reached for the photo, picked it up and raised her eyes to meet Adam's.

"You didn't take it. I did. This morning," he answered. "I had to be sure it was really Max before I mentioned it to Nathan."

"But how did you find him?" she asked in bewilderment.

"I went to see the house you used to live in," he said, and then cleared his throat. "I thought that, maybe, if I could picture what your life with Dan was like...." He paused.

Hot tears stung her eyes as she listened. "But Adam...." Her voice faltered. She didn't want to discuss what life with Dan had been like. Not even with Adam.

He continued in a somber voice. "Anyway, I found your old address in Heather's file here at the center, and I decided to take a look." He nodded toward the photo. "I saw that dog running around in the backyard there. Nathan had told me about Max—that he'd run away. He believes it's his fault for not taking good enough care of him."

"It wasn't his fault," Angela said. "It was Dan's.

I didn't know Nathan felt responsible. He's never mentioned that to me." Her heart sank. She thought she'd done a good thing by not telling the boy the reason Max had run off. Now to find out that Nathan had felt guilty all this time nearly broke her heart all over again.

"From what I could recall of Nathan's description, I thought that dog could be Max. I called out his name, and he came running."

"What did you do? Where is he?"

"I went up to the house and talked to the couple that live there. The man said the dog comes around every now and then. He feeds it and then it's gone again. No one seemed to claim him, so I took him with me. He's at the vet's clinic right now. They're cleaning him up and giving him whatever shots he needs."

"Oh, Adam," she breathed, "Nathan will be so happy. Thank you." She closed the distance between them in a quick step or two and gave him a spontaneous hug of gratitude. It was only when his strong arms moved to fully encircle her in the familiar warmth that she realized what a chance she'd taken. She hadn't seen him, touched him in such a long time. How was she supposed to let go now?

Adam held her close, in all her softness and warmth, as he struggled with the choice he faced—now, with this woman in his arms. Fight to keep her, or let her go? "Angie, tell me what Dan did that scared Max away."

She swallowed hard, trying to comprehend what he

was asking. And why. "He came home in the early hours of the morning and startled the dog. So naturally, Max growled and barked at him to protect me."

"And Dan did what? Hit him? Kicked him?" he asked without needing to. He already had a pretty good image in his mind.

Angela lifted her head to meet his silvery gaze. "Yes." She studied the sadness she saw in his eyes. "Why?"

"God, forgive me." He spoke gently and raised a hand to touch her face, loving her more now than ever before. "I don't want you to fear something like that happening again—not with me." He paused. "Find your kids, Angie, and go home."

She stared at him, stunned by his words. He had brought her down here to say that? Go home? "Adam, what's wrong? What does this have to do with seeing my old house today?" She couldn't understand what might have prompted such a change of heart. But what she didn't know was that if there had been a change of heart, it was only that he loved her *more.* The real change was in his thinking. "Think of what you've been through," he said.

"I don't want to think about it—"

"You have to. Before you let history repeat itself. You and the kids—you didn't know what time Dan was coming home, or some nights even if he was coming home at all. Your children couldn't even have a dog in the house in peace. Those are pretty basic things in life, Angie. I think you're entitled to them." He paused, but the sadness remained.

"But, Adam—"

"I shouldn't have dated you. I wouldn't have asked you out if I'd known the history you'd had with Dan." Adam looked away from her watery blue eyes and the obvious love shining there. "You're right to be afraid of a future with me. I don't think I'll ever take another drink again as long as I live, but even after seven years I can't promise you that." Angela listened to his words and felt him pulling away, gently, slowly. Her mind swirled with doubts and questions. She should be the one letting go. Not Adam. Not like this. She was the one who should say goodbye. *"What God finds acceptable, don't you call unacceptable."* The words from yesterday burned into her heart, but were they enough? For her or for Adam? Sure, he had become a Christian, and God had accepted him. But did that mean she should have no regard for his past? Or his alcoholism? It wouldn't go away just because he'd accepted Christ. Couldn't the Lord show her which path she should take? Was it all up to her? "Adam, things are different with you. You wouldn't—"

"You don't know what I'd do. I don't even know for sure what I'd do if I started drinking again." He walked away from her, sliding his hands into his pockets and shrugging his shoulders in defeat. "I stood looking at that house today, thinking of the pretty wife and three children that had lived there in what could have been a nice home for a happy family." He hesitated, trying to find the right words. "But it wasn't, was it?" He looked up to see Angela's eyes flood with tears. She shook her head. No. It hadn't been a happy family, and he wasn't going to let himself be the next man to hurt her. "A life with me wouldn't be fair to you. I don't want you to live in fear of something like that again."

"But you're not like Dan," Angela said in heartfelt honesty. "I wouldn't wonder whether or not you'd come home to me."

He stared at her, startled to hear her thoughts spoken aloud. Not come home to her? That was unimaginable. Some days, some nights…that was all he wanted in life. "Angie, don't." How he wished she wouldn't make this more difficult now that he'd determined to let her go. "You were right to run from me…from what I could be."

"It's not what I want," she said hesitantly, torn by conflicting emotions. "But Adam, it's just that…I don't know what to do. I keep thinking that the Lord will make it clear to me, but He hasn't. And if I walk out of here tonight, I know I'll be giving you up forever…completely. No more tomorrows…no more possibilities for us. And I'm not ready to do that—not yet." Her voice broke off in a soft cry. "Oh, Lord, I don't know how I'm ever going to do that." Her hand flew to cover her mouth.

Adam's heart ached for her in a way that it never had before. He reached out as she buried her face in her hands, and the tenderness in his touch against her dark curls, her shoulders seemed almost unbearable. He drew her gently to him, into the warmth she'd never forgotten existed, there, in Adam's arms. And he never wanted to let her go. "Seven years, Angie," he murmured into the softness of her hair. "Years—not months, weeks, days. I don't know any other way to prove myself to you. It's the Lord that keeps me from drinking—we both know that—but still, we can't do this...we can't be together, if you won't trust me, too." And if she couldn't, he would walk away. Now. Tonight. Once and for all. He had to if he wanted to hang on to his sanity. "When you said you wouldn't marry me, I didn't start drinking. I didn't give it up for you, and I won't go back to it when you leave—*if* you leave."

Angela wanted to trust, almost more than she wanted to breathe. Why couldn't she have some sign from the Lord? Some thought...*anything* that would make the choice clear to her? Prayer had not given her the answer she wanted. She wasn't asking for a fire in the sky or a voice from heaven. Just something other than her unquenchable love for this man.

Then Adam remembered Rob's suggestion. He'd been reluctant to use her brother's idea. It seemed a little "holier than thou" to him; but now he was running out of time and words...and hope. "What God finds acceptable, don't you call unacceptable." Adam's statement was quietly spoken, his lips brushing her temple with each syllable.

"What did you say?" Angela asked. Pulling away, she stared at him in wonder. She'd heard exactly what he'd said. Every word of it. The same words spoken in her Sunday School class yesterday morning. The teacher had looked directly at her, as if the message was meant for her alone. And hadn't she nearly dropped her coffee as she'd thought of Adam? If she needed any more of a sign than that, she would be asking for an out-and-out miracle. But then, wasn't that what this was? Her own personal miracle?

Adam didn't repeat what he'd said. He was lost in amazement that such a simple statement could bring such life to the tender blue of her eyes. Then he realized that he needed to respond. "It's something Rob said."

"Adam, that's it," she said in a hushed voice. "That's all we need." Then she was in his arms again, right where she belonged, and he held her close without understanding her sudden sense of confidence.

"Angie, why is that enough? And how could your brother know it would be?"

"The Lord told me that very thing—'What God finds acceptable, don't you call unacceptable'—in Sunday School yesterday. The teacher looked right at me when she said it." Angela laughed a little. "We were studying the tenth chapter of Acts—Peter and Cornelius and the visions, but I knew it was meant for us. I knew it immediately. In fact, I nearly dropped the cup of coffee I was holding!"

"Then why didn't you come to me yesterday? Why didn't you tell me?"

"Adam, you know me better than that. You don't think I'd trust myself to come to that conclusion, do you? I would probably have forgotten about it eventually if you hadn't said it. But that's all the confirmation I need. Rob couldn't possibly have known. The Lord has led him to that thought. Just for us, Adam, just for us.'' Angela lifted her head to study his face. Had she ever found anything less than she hoped for in this man's eyes? And how much hurt had she inflicted? ''Adam, I'm so sorry.''

But Adam moved his hand from the hollow of her back to press warm, strong fingers against her lips. He shook his head, unable to speak through the emotion. Was it possible to love someone too much? If so, he was certainly tumbling over that edge down to wherever it would lead. And he hoped God would forgive him because he wasn't looking for a way to turn back now. ''Angie, just say you'll marry me. Soon.''

''I will,'' she answered as she stared into his tender eyes, ''and it couldn't be soon enough—unless it happened right now.''

Adam's smile of satisfaction was brief. Then, with the gentle touch of his hands upon her face, he leaned close and Angela slowly raised herself up, meeting him halfway in the warmth of a kiss they'd gone too long without. In that moment, Adam knew—they both knew—their need of each other was unending. It took the quiet but persistent knock at the office door to bring their deepening kiss to a halt.

''Mom?'' Nathan pushed the door open a little, just enough to peek inside and see Angela in Adam's arms, smiling. And Nathan smiled in return. ''Does this mean things are okay with you two?'' he asked, a ring of uncertainty in his voice.

"*Very* okay," Angela said with confidence. "We're getting married. Soon."

"Honest? For real?"

"Honest. For real," she assured him. "And Adam has another piece of news you might enjoy hearing." Angela looked at Adam and nodded toward the photograph. "Show him."

"I guess I'll have to let go of you to do that," Adam stated, a mischievous slant to his mouth.

"Only for a moment." She smiled tenderly.

"You'll see this guy in person tomorrow, Nathan. For now, this will have to do." Adam reached for the photo and handed it to the boy.

"*Max!* Mom, is it really?"

"Yes. Adam went to our old house, and saw Max hanging around there, probably hoping to find you," Angela explained as Adam's arms went back around her. "Nathan, believe me, Max didn't run away because of anything you did. You had nothing to do with it at all."

"But can I see him? Can I keep him?" Nathan asked immediately. "David! Heather! Check this out!" He turned to his siblings who were crowding their way past him and into Adam's office. "It's Max!"

"We'll pick him up at the vet's tomorrow and bring him home," Adam explained.

"But we can't keep him at the apartment, Mom. You said we weren't allowed."

"Max can stay with me until your mother and I

are married. Then we're going to need to find a larger home,'' Adam told them.

''Married?'' Heather and David repeated in unison.

''Yes, married. Finally,'' Angela answered. ''But when?'' She met Adam's gentle gaze as Nathan showed the picture of Max and told his brother and sister what had happened.

''As soon as we can arrange it. We'll call Rob.''

''How about Thanksgiving?'' she suggested. ''Hopefully, Rob and Micah will be there with the babies. That would be wonderful, Adam. A wedding on Thanksgiving Day—a wedding we need to thank the Lord for. There couldn't be a more appropriate time.''

Adam smiled and pulled her close, brushing her temple with a light, teasing kiss. ''Sounds perfect.'' As perfect as life itself seemed in that moment. Adam and Angela both knew there would be much to be grateful for this Thanksgiving Day. And every day thereafter.

Epilogue

"Dearly beloved, we are gathered together...."

"*...to ask the Lord's blessing. He chastens and hastens, His will to make known.*" Heather's happy voice burst into song, singing a portion of the musical selection she'd performed at school in last night's Thanksgiving program. Everyone that had crowded into the Granston living room for the wedding looked at her, first in surprise and then with quiet amusement.

"Thank you, Heather," Rob said from where he stood close to the fireplace. "You're right. We are here to ask the Lord's blessing."

"Especially on Thanksgiving, Uncle Rob."

"True enough, hon, but what I was aiming for was 'to join this man and this woman in holy matrimony.'" Rob exchanged a gentle look with his sister, who stood before him, in a delicate ivory suit, beside her husband-to-be.

Micah, Hope and Grace were all smiling broadly

at Heather's enthusiasm. The little girl was obviously too excited about the wedding to keep silent. And she was right: it was a day specifically set aside to thank the Lord for his goodness.

"What's a wedding without a little music?" Adam suggested, and squeezed Angela's hand.

"Go ahead." Heather's wide blue eyes gazed up at her uncle, the minister. "That's your job. Marry them. Then maybe I'll sing something else...if you really want me to, Adam."

Adam assured her that it was what he and Angela *both* wanted, and the ceremony proceeded. The school principal married the recreation director in the midst of family, friends and the crying of the Granston twins, who woke up before the wedding was over that Thanksgiving noon. Then the holiday was truly observed at Ed and Grace Granston's home with prayer offered over a traditional turkey dinner that was enjoyed by everyone present. Even Micah, who quite proudly displayed to Angela her newly acquired skills of feeding, burping and changing diapers on her two tiny babies—without most of the fear she'd exhibited earlier.

"You're doing fine with them, Micah," Angela said. "Just like I knew you would. But let Rob help you as much as he can."

"I'm still worried that I'll do something wrong, but I'm taking it one day at a time, and so far I'm doing okay. And Rob does help me a lot," she added. "I don't think I could handle this without him. He even takes care of the middle-of-the-night feedings so I can get some sleep." She paused, then laughed quietly. "Lucky for you I have him around. Otherwise, I might be calling you for help and interrupting your honeymoon."

Angela glanced across the room toward the fireplace where Adam stood talking with her father and Eric. At that moment he looked over at her and smiled, watching her as he listened to his new brother-in-law. Angela squeezed Micah's arm and leaned close to whisper, "Call Mom or Hope. I don't want to hear from anyone until Monday."

Micah nodded and promised not to bother the newlyweds—no matter what happened during the long holiday weekend.

Angela looked at the tranquil scene just outside the living room window of Adam's home. Crisp white snow covered the ground with more fat flakes floating from the sky as she watched. The reflection of the street light on the sparkling snow made the lovely picture all the more mesmerizing. And her new diamond flashed in the dim light of the room with even the slightest movement of her hand. Her kids would dig out the sleds tomorrow from where they'd been stored in the garage during the past two years of minimal snowfall. This would be the winter weekend of their dreams. Angela smiled. Hers, too, but it had nothing to do with the weather. Three days and nights alone with Adam were more than she'd hoped for during this busy time of year. The fire crackled in the wood-burner in the corner, adding to the perfect scenario for their time alone together. She turned from the window at the sound of his footsteps.

"Hi," she said quietly, wrapping her hands around the mug of hot chocolate Adam offered her. "Looks good," she commented and studied Adam's smile through the shadows.

"So do you," he answered. He placed his cup on the nearby end table, then touched the shoulder of her satiny gown. "Although I kind of miss that baggy sweat suit you were wearing the night we first met."

"You'll see plenty of that when we're back home with the kids."

"I didn't realize you'd come out of the bedroom," Adam remarked as he glanced through the window at the wintry scene. "It's nearly 1:00 a.m. I thought maybe you'd fallen asleep."

"Not a chance, my husband," she replied. Then she placed her cup on the end table next to his, freeing her hands to slide around his waist and settle comfortably behind him against the belt of his brown robe. "I may never sleep again."

Adam's smile widened. "My thoughts exactly." He leaned forward to kiss the tip of her nose. "I love you, Angie."

"And I love you." She relaxed into his waiting embrace. They stood together in the shadowy silence of the darkened room, watching the holiday snowfall.

"Let it snow, let it snow, let it snow." Angela whispered the words to one of her daughter's favorite tunes. But the weather had nothing to do with Angela's predictions for the coming days—or nights. For her, it would be a warm December.

* * * * *

Dear Reader,

Thank you for choosing my book! It's fun to write stories of love and commitment about people seeking God's plan for their lives. The Love Inspired® line offers books filled with the "forever" kind of romance we all want to believe in. When *A Wedding in the Family* begins, young widow Angela Sanders doesn't hold out much hope of a true love for a lifetime; but when the possibility materializes in the form of Adam Dalton, Angela is caught off guard. She's not at all certain she wants to accept the risks involved. It's only when she realizes God's affirmation of her love for Adam that she can allow the happy ending for herself…the one she'd thought she'd never find. I think you'll be happy for her.

I've loved writing stories for as long as I can remember. Having an opportunity to share this one with you is a gift to me from the Lord. Years ago, during a time of discouragement, I was told by a successful author that God wouldn't have given me this desire to write without supplying a place for me to use it. Steeple Hill's Love Inspired® line is that place. I hope you enjoy my work.

Kathryn Alexander

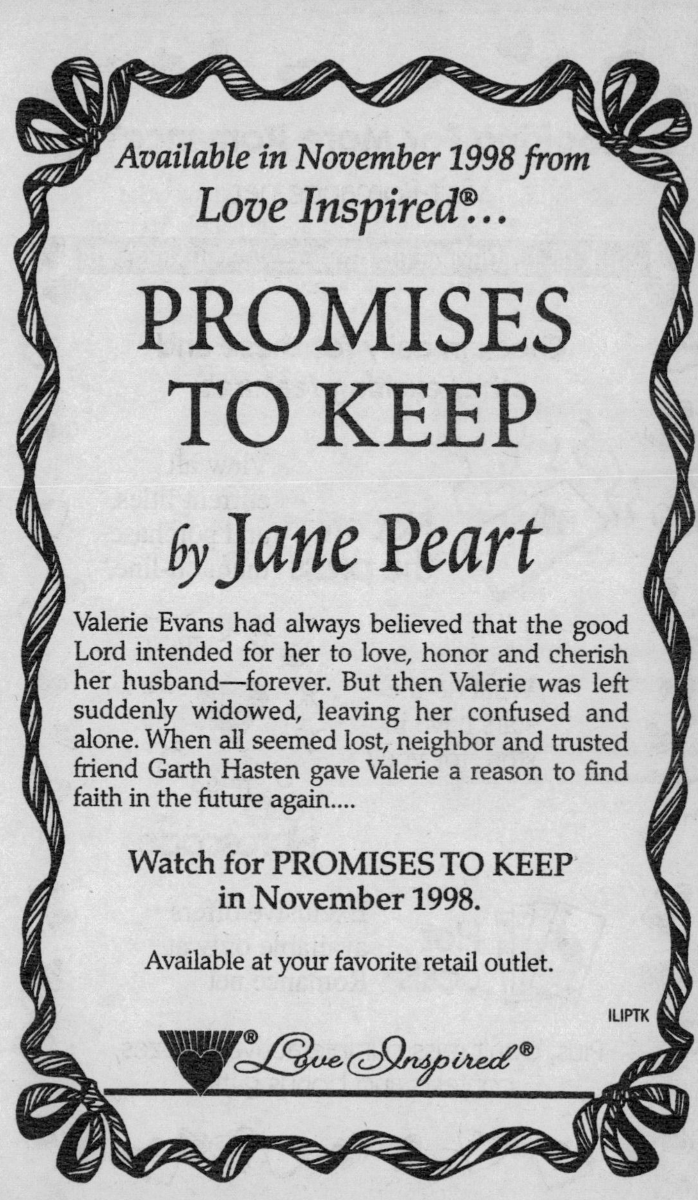

Available in November 1998 from
Love Inspired®...
PROMISES
TO KEEP
by Jane Peart
Valerie Evans had always believed that the good Lord intended for her to love, honor and cherish her husband—forever. But then Valerie was left suddenly widowed, leaving her confused and alone. When all seemed lost, neighbor and trusted friend Garth Hasten gave Valerie a reason to find faith in the future again....
Watch for PROMISES TO KEEP
in November 1998.
Available at your favorite retail outlet.
ILIPTK
Love Inspired®

Looking For More Romance?
Visit Romance.net
Look us up on-line at: http://www.romance.net
Check in daily for these and other exciting features:
Hot off the press
View all current titles, and purchase them on-line.
What do the stars have in store for you?
Horoscope
Hot deals
Exclusive offers available only at Romance.net
Plus, don't miss our interactive quizzes, contests and bonus gifts.
PWEB

Available in November 1998 from
Love Inspired®...
TWO RINGS,
ONE HEART
by Martha Mason
Mitch Whitney returned to his family looking for forgiveness. Finally he felt emotionally ready to take on his responsibilities as father and husband. However, would his family be ready to accept him back into their lives? A woman of strong faith, Megan had never stopped loving Mitch, but could she learn to trust him again?
Available at your favorite retail outlet.
Love Inspired®
ILI2R

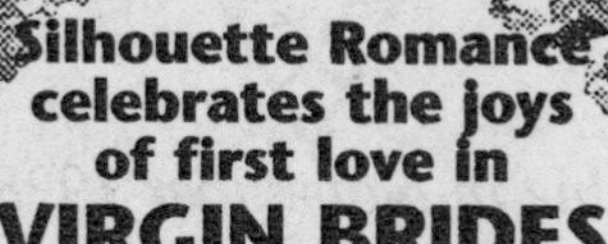

September 1998:
THE GUARDIAN'S BRIDE
by Laurie Paige (#1318)

A young heiress, desperately in love with her older, wealthy guardian, dreams of wedding the tender tycoon. But he has plans to marry her off to another....

October 1998:
THE NINE-MONTH BRIDE
by Judy Christenberry (#1324)

A widowed rancher who wants an heir and a prim librarian who wants a baby decide to marry for convenience—but will motherhood make this man and wife rethink their temporary vows?

November 1998:
A BRIDE TO HONOR by Arlene James (#1330)

A pretty party planner falls for a charming, honor-bound millionaire who's being roped into a loveless marriage. When the wedding day arrives, will *she* be his blushing bride?

December 1998:
A KISS, A KID AND A MISTLETOE BRIDE (#1336)

When a scandalous single dad returns home at Christmas, he encounters the golden girl he'd fallen for one magical night a lifetime before.

Available at your favorite retail outlet.

Look us up on-line at: http://www.romance.net

SRVBSD